I0819656

THE LANGUAGE OF LIARS

ALSO BY S. L. HUANG

The Water Outlaws

Burning Roses

CAS RUSSELL SERIES

Zero Sum Game

Null Set

Critical Point

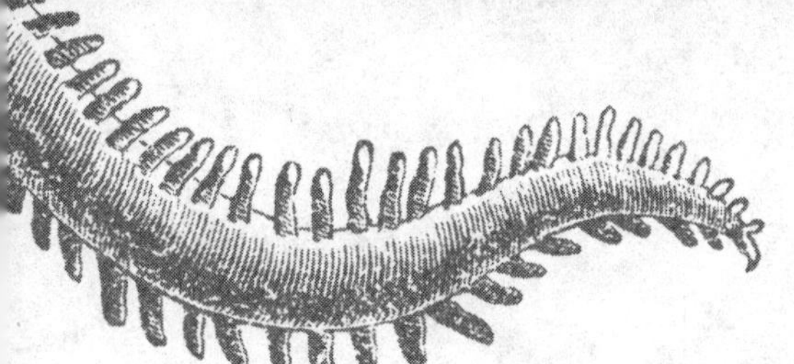

THE LANGUAGE OF LIARS

S. L. HUANG

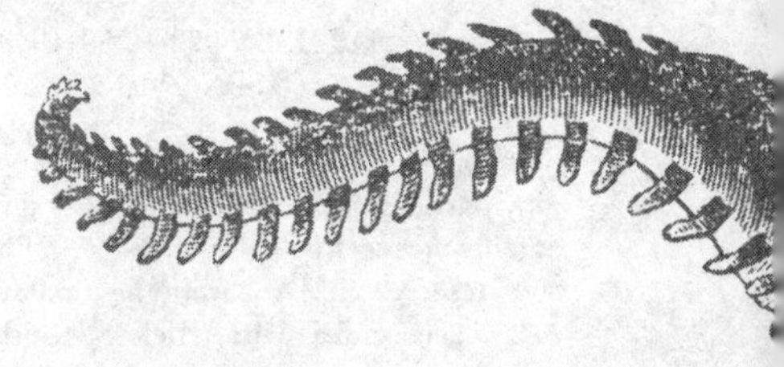

TOR PUBLISHING GROUP
NEW YORK

This is a work of fiction. All of the names, characters, organizations, places, and events portrayed in this work are either products of the author's imagination or used fictitiously.

THE LANGUAGE OF LIARS

A Tordotcom Book
Published by Tom Doherty Associates / Tor Publishing Group
120 Broadway
New York, NY 10271

www.torpublishinggroup.com

EU Representative: Macmillan Publishers Ireland Ltd, 1st Floor, The Liffey Trust Centre, 117–126 Sheriff Street Upper, Dublin 1, D01 YC43

The Library of Congress Cataloging-in-Publication Data is available upon request.

ISBN 978-1-250-40533-3 (hardcover)
ISBN 978-1-250-40534-0 (ebook)

First Edition: 2026

Printed in the United States of America

10 9 8 7 6 5 4 3 2 1

dedication (noun)

ded·i·ca·tion, /ˌdɛdɪˈkeɪʃən/

1: reserving for a specific use

the dedication of an entire page for something that's usually only one line, to emphasize its gravity and meaning

2: commitment, devotion, or loyalty

reflecting the dedication of a friendship filled with irreplaceable decades of conversation and ideas, math, language, philosophy, and adventures in three countries

3: tribute message affixed to a literary or other artistic work

the dedication of this book to Linda Brown

4: event marking completion of a building, ship, or other project (*see also: opening ceremony, ribbon cutting*)

with whom I will someday break a champagne bottle over the prow of a ship in its first dedication, then together sail to the stars, because who are we to question the dictionary

CONTENTS

THE LANGUAGE OF LIARS

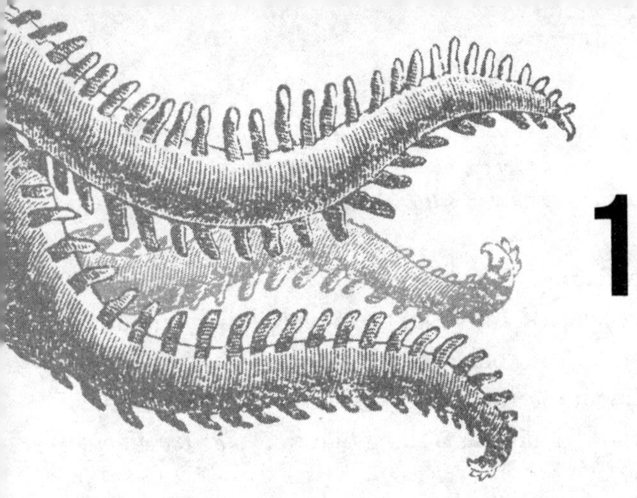

1

Nineteen Words for Doubt. Twenty-Six Ways to Lie.

At first the Orro Primaries were skeptical.

"Language causes the mind to jump?" they said.

"No. Understanding causes the jump. Language is the tool," said the Master Linguist.

"This ability would make us feared. It will only give us trouble from the conglomerate," said the Primaries.

"No," said the Master Linguist. "It will give us spies."

—Orro Internal Records, Dissolution Era
(labeled for destruction)

The day Ro jumped was the first day he doubted.

Doubt. In his language, it meant uncertainty, apprehension, a lack of confidence or conviction. The feeling of a squiggle in his third and fourth stomachs.

In Birjivina, the trade language of the Andu-Erjians, *doubt* meant a question—either a question raised or a question asked. Andu-Erjians said things like *Ask your doubts* or

We have seventeen doubts to settle about this treaty with the Gendamese.

The Gendamese had twenty-two common languages across three species. In one of them, everything could be made negative. You could have *minus doubt*, which roughly meant self-assurance or security. Another of their tongues used the word "doubt" as a slang question tag: *You get me, doubt? Undoubt.*

The Koi people had only one language and didn't name it. Why did you need a name for something self-evident? The closest concept to "doubt" in their language roughly meant "miasma." They didn't have words for abstract concepts; they had sensory metaphors. You weren't *happy*, you were *the sound of trilling*. You weren't *in love*, you were *enveloped by warmth*. "Sound" and "warmth" themselves were odd translations, since both species of the Koi had cell splinters that would break apart not very far above absolute zero—the literal translation of *warmth* was a numerical measurement a fraction of a degree above nothing. Warm to the Koi, perhaps, but a death sentence to most other species in the conglomerate.

Except the Star Eaters.

The Star Eaters—those most studied, and least known. Beings born of nebula and cold vacuum.

The Star Eaters had at least nineteen gestural words and phrases that meant some variation of doubt. *Doubt of place. Doubt of identity. Doubt of purpose . . .*

Ro scuffed against the clay where he lay claw-curled on the surface—not *precisely* hiding from his teachers—and hitched himself around to snuff at the hazy sky. None of those words meant his own people's concept of doubt, not really. Their learning at the Warren stressed it over and over: *Language is unpaired.* It will not match like a converted measurement. Only clouds of overlapping colored meaning that, in their shifting, might briefly end up combining to form *almost* the same hue as a word or phrase or gesture or semantic unit in the other language.

That seemed obvious to Ro, but his Seniors didn't like him saying so.

They also didn't like him skipping meditation or answering his milestone testing in a dialect of Haazgi. In Ro's defense, he *tried* to remember to meditate, but he and schedules had never gotten on well, and he often remembered his good intentions a half night past when he meant to go. And he truly hadn't been trying to caper when he wrote in Haazgi! He'd just been trying to think in it as practice, and it was such a common trade record that it hadn't occurred to him that most of the Seniors *couldn't* read it. They were Senior Linguists, weren't they? Why wouldn't he assume they knew more than he did?

That hadn't been the way they took it.

Skipping meditation or training wasn't supposed to be against the rules anyway. The Warren had never had a rule slate before Ro's fifth cycle here—*Warren recruits are too self-motivated to need rules*, had been the lofty claim.

Until me, Ro thought. He was always tripping up people's good opinions without meaning to.

Of late the Seniors kept *pushing* at him mentally, their emotions a looming shadow in the corner of his empathic sense. The type of shadow that meant, *We need to have a serious talk with you, Ro,* where "serious" meant unpleasantness and sour faces and hot dollops of shame. Hence the hiding.

Ro liked the surface more than most of his people did. With any luck the Seniors might fail to seek him up here, as they flinched from the open space and the bright, without Ro appearing to avoid them. He'd *tried* to scrape himself into going to training today, but every bristle of his fur shivered away from that towering judgment, only releasing once he'd scurried up here and pattered in circles against the hardness and dust.

Acceptance at the Warren had been what was supposed to finally let him prove himself. An Orro Linguist, for real! After so many sighs and disappointed snufflings from his hive elders . . . When Ro was a youngling, those elders had sometimes referred to him by a nickname that roughly meant *cheerful disaster.* Affectionately, of course. And sometimes right after exclaiming over his potential, the way he gobbled new words and new tongues so eagerly (*"A Linguist! Do you think? Could he be?"*). But Ro couldn't deny how often he found himself befuddled after ending topsy-turvy on what everyone else did with no effort, like scraping lichen without making a mess, or remembering which tunnel he wanted, or keeping his fur from getting sticky again and poking up every which way . . . To then be selected for the most prestigious, the most respected studies on all Orro! It had felt like putting all the rest behind him, the chance to *show* himself worthy.

Once he learned what the Warren trained for in truth, that determination had only rocketed.

Jumping. Orro's largest and most bewitching secret.

Ro was resolved to be the first Linguist in generations to make a jump. If he worked hard enough, with both hearts behind it, and remembered to log his training properly instead of getting carried away with untangling ghost consonants in ancient Kerkard . . .

He could remember to do all that. Mostly, at least.

And so Ro had thrown himself into gaining a full linguistic understanding of the Star Eaters. Enough for those dancing colors of unpaired meaning in *his* mind to find a match, just for a blink. One precious beat of him, an outsider, syncing with some nameless Star Eater out in the black—a crystalline pulse of matched understanding. Language was the tool: a language just alien enough, a learned secondary language that would cast one's mind in a mold just different enough, for that perfect alignment to snap his people's empathic neurology against the mind of another being.

How fabulous! One thought, fully subsumed in another's words as a native mind would perceive them. Speaking from their perspective in a perfect fluent paradigm. One thought different enough from Ro's base linguistic patterns, from his own learned language paths, and instead resonant with another in the same moment.

That was what it took, to trigger a jump.

The power of language. Ro marveled at it regularly. The meditation, the study, everything the Warren had built around—it all aimed toward that singular goal, that one moment.

That one moment was, admittedly, near impossible. In the history of the Warren, not more than three Linguists in any generation had managed to jump into another mind this way. For many cycles now, none had. The unique neurology of the Ponto species might make such an ability possible—but not easy.

Ro ruffled his fur against the clay and closed his eyes, imagining again how it might feel. That quick pure fluidity in another mind's point of view . . . it would yank his consciousness instantly, imprinting him lightyears away in the body of a Star Eater. His chance to study their intricate, full-body communication and poignant, tragedy-soaked history and culture—to *really study it.* To *understand* in a way no outsider ever could.

How could such a thing not be any Linguist's double-heart desire?

Admittedly, some of his compatriots couldn't handle the idea. They washed out of the Warren, sworn to secrecy. The prospect of a one-way trip away from their hives, away from their homes—it proved too much for them.

Those were the minority. Most trainees stayed. And trained. And yearned.

And failed.

Ro had never conceived that he might fail.

The Warren had felt such a paradise at first. A place where Ro would finally, naturally *fit.* He'd quickly shot past most of his colleagues on the language study—by so much that their auras chafed with an angular and unhidden envy. Ro, exuberant to at last be among classmates who would understand him, had attempted to defuse such tension by offering mnemonic tricks or delicious facts, or to earn wriggles of amusement through multilingual wordplay. Too late he caught on that his peers, like his Seniors, only interpreted it as arrogance.

(How could he explain that excitedly sharing an Oltasol and Yotz mixed pun was the opposite of arrogance? He thought they'd get it! And, more importantly, it had been funny.)

Niggles in the back of his mind began to chew at him sometimes. To make a jump was also to adapt, to excel at all the small life challenges that Ro so regularly stumbled over. What if his Seniors thought he couldn't handle that part?

He would just have to stay good enough at the language bits. Jumping would make up for whatever else his Seniors sighed at. It would make up for Ro, eclipse any deficiencies with the magnitude of his service to Orro.

If he could make it.

The *miasma* of Ro's continued lack of success had begun stalking him over every recent revolution of their moon. Most Linguists who had managed the jump had done it young. Ro was barely an adult, not even at second molt yet—his peers who hadn't been recruited to serve Orro would only now be embarking on lives outside their hives at his age. But he imagined he could feel his mind becoming less flexible by the day, resisting that conceptual malleability.

What if he couldn't do it? What would be his worth to anyone?

He wouldn't say he *doubted*, though. Not yet.

He felt his Senior's neurological aura before any other sense: a pulse of high discipline and exacting organization that made him twist around. Senior Aga. They'd found him.

He resisted the urge to scamper away. Senior Aga would

have felt him too by now, was clearly up here seeking him. A moment later his Senior's distinctive stride stumped around the clay brick of the nearest entrance mound—Senior Aga tended to walk on three legs instead of two or four, swinging one foreleg down to lope lopsided unless carrying something. And today with an aura that seared brittle at the edges, a sharp tang that Ro could feel directed at himself.

He scrambled to uncurl and straighten, pressing his paw pads apart on the ground in nervous habit.

Ro's studies had once included a foreign analysis of the empathic sense that had been normal to him since birth. The outside researcher had marveled at the transparency, the intimacy, the inability to lie when one's emotions were on such full display. *Their language does not have a word for lying, as there is no such concept*, the author had claimed.

So incorrect as to be comedy! Ro's species—the Ponto—had spread among at least seven different domains of the conglomerate, every one of which had some cultural concept of falsehood, including Ro's home of Orro. Originally a small colony of the Ponto homeworld, on a settlement moon they still shared with others, Orro remained ninety-seven percent Ponto—and their eponymous mother tongue included plenty of words for untruth. It simply had no *paired* word. Ro's native speech labeled *socially kind, harmless untruth* as different from *political spinning into untruth*, which was again different from *intentional, targeted untruth meant to distort what is felt or real.* That last one could be a serious crime on Orro—enough for offenders to be removed from their hives for their loved ones' safety.

Mental auras were like facial expressions, or postures,

or ripples of fur; they gave away some things and hid others. Such an odd misapprehension, to think they couldn't lie!

Ro's Senior was coming straight for him, claws clicking against the hard-packed ground. Ro marshalled his mind away from scattering on linguistic factoids, soothing his own aura. He hadn't *technically* broken any rules . . .

"I see you, Senior," he offered in polite rote greeting.

"Seen," Senior Aga grunted.

The disapproval reeked at Ro in waves. He flexed his paw pads against the ground, trying to keep the motion small.

"You missed training again with no log," Senior Aga said. "What are you doing up here?"

"Meditating," Ro lied.

An untruth that is adjacent enough one can pretend. An untruth of self. His aura would show consternation, but not the lie.

Senior Aga gave the too-familiar huff of disappointment. "I have defended you."

Ro couldn't help his flash of surprise.

"The Seniors have long shown laxness toward your lapses in attendance and required study, far beyond what many believed wise. I have reminded my colleagues that we impress upon all of you how one cannot jump merely from preparatory reading, that *doing* is the only way. How using the language must be the greatest share of time. Your dedication to that, at least, has been impossible to dispute."

Ro's dread swelled. He'd practically lived in the practice cocoons before his worries began to gnaw. Lately, however . . .

He hated failing again. It hurt.

"Your hours in the cocoons have dropped inexcusably. It has not gone unnoticed." The ridges above Senior Aga's eyes dipped in severity. "Are you ill?"

Ill could have a large meaning here: *ill, disturbed, struggling.*

"No, Senior," Ro lied. *A partial untruth, a technical untruth.* He was not ill. He ignored the broader shape of the word.

"You have great potential. But potential is nothing unless it can be realized."

Ro's fur spiked and stung. "I know—"

"Do you? The resources of the Warren do not exist for you to *play* at being a Linguist, Trainee."

"I—I'll go to the cocoons today," Ro managed.

"See that you do."

Senior Aga's long, flat nostrils huffed and snuffed for a moment, shoulder fur rippling . . . that same long-suffering expression that Ro had seen so many times before. Then the older Ponto loped past and toward the staff tunnels for the fully trained Warren Linguists—the ones who hadn't jumped.

Some still tried. Others seemed resigned to their evolved positions, as researchers and revered advisors to their government's Primaries. And naturally, they also donned the mantle of sculpting new, young recruits toward the ultimate service to Orro.

Like one of Ro's elder hive mothers. Mother Hobi. Several generations above him, she'd been his favorite hive elder—he'd followed her around as a youngling, begging for new words, new ideas, and she'd delighted in obliging him. Following in her footprints had been his greatest ambition.

As far back as Ro could remember, Mother Hobi had been esteemed by the rest of the hive as an Orro Linguist. It wasn't until Ro learned the secrets of the Warren that he realized she was an unsuccessful one.

The tricklings of guilt reminded him how his view of her had changed. He'd assumed so easily—that *he* would prove himself where she had not, that *his* path would take him to the stars.

How had she coped?

Ro cast about for any sense of Senior Aga, but his Senior was gone, aura indistinguishable among the bubbling of life in the tunnels. Ro had promised he would go to the practice cocoons today. But he hadn't said he would go *right now.*

He twisted, dropped to all fours, and scuttled in the opposite direction.

Orro's tunnels didn't have firm boundaries between their uses like some urban areas Ro had visited. A much smaller body politic than most in the conglomerate, Orro itself wasn't much beyond a single large population center—what the Faomish League called a *city-state* or what the Zayallayi called a *micro-world. World*, of course, was a misnomer, given that Orro shared this moon and its spaceports with territories under thirty-seven other governments. But language wasn't mindful of such literal definitional mappings.

(Except for the Lukyusi language, of the Baihyan people, which was painfully literal, and defined anything else as a lie. A single-species people, the Baihyan had a physiological stress reaction to any meaning that strayed. Funny that Ro's people got labeled the ones who couldn't lie. But then, the Baihyan had a single word for it.)

Ro padded along beneath the haze-pale sky, past where the Warren's tunnels phased into leadership halls beneath his feet. The lonely emptiness of the surface paths cradled his moroseness. The atmosphere was high today, and light air pops puffed against his fur occasionally. With a population of less than seven million, Orro sprawled among the dusty northern mountains and was able to comfortably house everyone by urbanizing mostly straight downward. Which meant the space near and on the surface had plenty of room for government offices—more comfortable for their less subterranean neighbors to visit—as well as gardens and public surface parks and the aboveground transportation hubs.

It wouldn't take long to get to this ward's lift. It never took very long to get anywhere on Orro.

One geothermally assisted capsule tumble later, Ro rolled out near the back of his family's hive, two hundred layers down. His nostrils flared with the familiarity of the damp mineral scent he'd been born to. He could sense his aura vibrating. He rolled his paw pads against the cool grit of the rock floor.

When was the last time he'd been home? He'd thought at first that he should see them as much as possible before he jumped, soak in the love of his hive. He would miss them dearly, but who could say no to such a chance?

Only later had crept the sneaking apathy. *If I can jump, I won't see them anymore anyway. Best to distance myself. Isn't it?*

And then, the dribbles of shame: *I'm still here. I shouldn't still be here.*

His family didn't know that. But Mother Hobi would. She'd know he was failing, like she had.

He was suddenly desperate to see her.

"Ro!" Lalo's aura burst onto him as she tumbled out of one of the tunnels. "I felt you coming! Coro and Sa are going to be so happy, they said they've sent you a whole canyon full of voice bubbles. Why have you been so long!"

"Just busy," Ro lied. *A face-saving lie, for privacy.* But his fur couldn't help cresting up in joy, his mood lifting. "I see you, Lalo."

"*Seen.*" She said it with an exaggerated quiver, a vivacious impatience with the pleasantries. "Now come *on*!"

She mauled her shoulder up against his and hustled them from the lift.

Ro let himself be hustled. Lalo's scent, like bright clean earth, and the texture of her fur, somehow both sleek and coarse against his—they carried him along the familiar, softly lit tunnels. Like the Warren, his hive had no firm boundaries—only Orro tunnels that became theirs at some juncture by virtue of them sprawling to live in and maintain them. Lalo wasn't the only one who had felt him arrive; his litter-sisters Coro and Sa barreled into him with excited trills, and then he was buried under an excited pile of family.

Lalo drew back a little then. Ro's awareness kept seeking her out, though he tried not to be obvious about it. Her aura was like a treasure nest, surprising and delighting in its bursts of vividness. Her strand of the hive had joined his when her thirdkin cousin traded bonds with one of Ro's firstkin, and about fifty of them had come along to join hive with Ro's. Ro had been about to leave for the Warren then, talking nothing but language—which languages have contranyms, and which are exceptions to the accepted etymological evolution for visual adjectives, and *Did you know it's this common for people to split differently from having one audio system and one visual system like writing, the Bash have five sensory representations of the same language!!*—until everyone but Mother Hobi gave him an exasperated nudge-off.

But Lalo had been fascinated.

Fascinated, and appallingly awful. She mangled the pronunciation of any word not her own and was prone to wrinkling her cheeks and saying things like, "But what do you *mean* I can't put the word *big* after the word *round* in Kuyqish because the vowels aren't friendly? I just did!"

And Ro's fur would go straight up, and he wouldn't know what to say except, "Because you can't!"

Then she'd say, "But *why*? I bet you there's some Kuyqish poet who does that *just to get her claws in people*," and he'd keep saying, "but you *can't*, it's disharmonious!" and then she'd go and look it up and find a Dissolution Era culture rebel who sang discomfort and shouted messages of love and peace in aggressively atonal discordance, and caused an entire generation of Kuyqish youth at the time to mix disharmonious vowels in slang.

And *then* she found the medical case studies of the ones who sustained nerve damage from it.

"Oh," she said. "I guess you can't."

Lalo was so different from Ro. She wanted to go space-ward and study exotic materials engineering. She'd chattered Ro's ears off about space skipping and the meridian element, and he'd let it wash over him like a different tongue.

Once the Warren pointed him toward the Star Eaters, though . . . then he'd paid much more avid attention.

Occasionally he'd even dared ask her careful questions, trying to keep his aura casual: *Why* is *it that scientists haven't been able to figure this out? Why is it only the Star Eaters?*, or *But if the meridian element is the only thing that can make bubbles of spacetime go faster than light, how can the Star Eaters sense it from across a galaxy?*

Doesn't that mean their senses go faster than light, too?

. . . isn't that impossible?

Lalo's fur would electrify and her whole aura would pop off in starbursts and she'd cry, "Oh oh oh, this is why it's smashing!"

He always tried very hard to follow at least half of what came next.

Lalo was so different from him . . . and so the same. The hive never knew quite what to do with her, either.

Ro had promised his Senior he'd put in practice time. But in the rowdy puddle of warmth that was his hive, he delayed going back, and delayed again. He let Mother Pogo ply him with mineral juice and freshly marinated lichens, and his youngest thirdkin proudly show off their twirl-rolling, and he claw-curled next to Lalo by a geotherm vent, bathing in her patter about the minimum number of meridian paths you'd need to visit the known galaxy.

He must have dozed off, because when he opened his

eyes Mother Hobi had replaced her. He couldn't sense anyone else nearby, their auras bobbing in the surrounding tunnels.

"I shooed them. So as not to wake you," Mother Hobi said. "I see you, Ro."

"I see you." Ro shifted, uncurling his claws from beneath him.

"*Se qetů?*" Mother Hobi asked quietly. Her nostrils huffed out wide and flat in sympathy.

Ro's fur riffled before he could stop it. The phrase was from Oltasol, the minority language on Orro—spoken mostly by non-Ponto and those they hived with and lagging far behind either Ponto or the trade pidgin in usage. The question was a phrase absent from Ro's native tongue, and it meant, roughly, *Share with me.*

No, it meant more than that. It meant she knew something was wrong, and it obligated a reply via her concern and connection. It was one of Oltasol's "undeniable phrases," the ones that defied any argument.

("They're not *undeniable,*" Lalo liked to say. "You can deny them all you want!" What she didn't understand was that the undeniable phrases more properly should have been translated as *disarming.* When someone said one to you, they were imbuing a meaning of having crossed over with you into a shared vulnerability. To refuse an undeniable phrase was to take that vulnerability and punch through it with a claw.)

Ro was not about to punch his closest hive mother in an undeniable phrase.

He did take his time in answering.

"*Se qetè ti pu qaifu?*" he whispered finally, into the vent's warmth. *What if I can't?*

Mother Hobi paused. Shifted. Then she said, in Ponto: "I hope you never make the jump."

Ro jerked around toward her. His aura must have reverberated like a shock wave.

Mother Hobi shouldered up against him, trapping him in her warmth like he was a youngling. "When I was your age, I was the same. Such ambition. Now I know that if I had gone . . . I would have missed everything."

"But the *keykka*!" It was a Nahonic word for *chance*, but bigger, backed by the cataclysm of incalculable loss.

"My young Ro. Perhaps the jump is 'keykka.' But so is what I have built here—the long stretches with the hive mothers, with you. That's keykka, too. I would not trade it."

"*Bchni*," Ro said promptly. From Pichto Creole: *impossible*. But mildly vulgar. Slang. Disbelieving.

"Wipe your tongue," Mother Hobi said, but she sounded amused. "I notice the way your aura bends around Lalo. You see keykka in the jump, so you think the choice is easy, but discarding all this—it would not be nothing for you. The chance to enter bonds, to raise the hive's next younglings, to build a vibrant life—even to continue learning and growing in your own skin, and not hiding your true self until you die . . . Our Primaries ask a great sacrifice. It would be very lonely, after a time."

"But worth it," Ro insisted. His resolve was kicking back in, reminding him of all the reasons to keep striving. "To be able to experience another culture that way? *Really* experience it? It's, it's incalculable!"

"It gives you no hesitation, the theft of another's self?"

Ro paused. That was the part he tried not to think about. As far as anyone knew from reports of the jumped Linguists, the leap took over the original Star Eater completely. At least for the Ponto lifetime.

"The reports all go silent eventually," Ro pointed out. "We're so much shorter-lived than a Star Eater. Chances are we're only borrowing."

"The great lie," Mother Hobi murmured.

She used the word that meant *a lie enough repeated until it becomes true.*

"They might not even care. They might not even *notice,*" Ro pressed on. "Their culture is so hard for us to comprehend! That's why we have to do this. We don't even know if they remember past the last confusion period. And it's not like I don't think about—but it's so few of them that we borrow, right? And for just a blink from their perspective. Isn't it worth both my life and theirs, to build these sorts of better understandings? Especially with the Star Eaters. Think what it could mean for our people, for *all* people!"

Mother Hobi was still nestled against him. "*Meámpīgl leù xài weāglwìm,*" she said.

A Hattadine proverb, usually translated as: *The young are able to believe.* Or sometimes: *To be young is to be sure.*

Ro told himself he was sure.

"I have to go back," he said.

Mother Hobi pressed her head against his for a long moment, then let him go.

The moon had rotated into second darkness by the time Ro returned to the surface, with only a sliver of reflected planetlight stretched in a dim curve against the sky. The conversation with Mother Hobi had reinvigorated a stubborn ambition. Ro had promised Senior Aga he'd visit the practice cocoons today, and practice he would, for sessions upon sessions upon sessions.

He trotted down to the Warren's astral hub, dust kicking up beneath the pads of his feet. The time had rolled late enough that few of the cocoons were in use. Only the most ambitious trainees still stayed.

Ro used to be one of those. He could be again. He would *resolve* to be again.

He wound the strings and wheels on one of the cocoons to set it for Star Eater. Not that the Warren trained them toward much else, these days. But sometimes trainees wanted to attempt Qwani, or Red Top, or one of the other languages the Warren had created astral pockets for that Ponto mouths and claws had little hope of practicing without chimeric help. Ro had spent his whole first cycle at the Warren ecstatically trying them all.

Remember why you love this. Why it matters.

Ro pressed the pads of his feet apart against the cold ground, then thrust his paws through the folds of the cocoon and plunged inside.

The Warren practice cocoons were one of the only places on Orro that could generate a full astral pocket. One sprang up instantly, grabbing hold of Ro's aura and overtaking every one of his senses. For the briefest of overlaps he could feel his Ponto body sinking into the yielding depths of the cocoon, then his Ponto self was gone.

He floated in a body of twisting sinew and sensitive cilia, no defined head, the cocoon giving him a vague scattering of patterns that mimicked sensory organs down each fanning tentacle. The scenario had placed him in space, as it often did. Other Star Eaters floated some distance from him, reflected in gently flaring lacework from some unseen sun, enormous filigree creatures of the black.

Simulations. Painted into his mind by the cocoon.

Ro tried to sink into the language without a ripple. He would go and speak to the simulations in a moment—first he sought to become of one mind with this constructed body of sensations, of speech without tongues. Normalizing its perceptions, considering the universe as a Star Eater might.

A residual consternation flickered down the cilia, in a very un-Star-Eater-like expression.

You'll never be able to jump like that. Think like them. Be of them!

This was why he was supposed to practice meditation, wasn't it? Ro forced himself into a rhythm and began reciting some rote phrases, in the Star Eaters' way: *work is life, work is work. baseline, baseline. unbothered.*

The muscle pulses and electromagnetic pops fell into cadence in a way that felt much more correct. One of the simulations began wafting toward him, and he prepared to engage in practice conversation with a fluent mind.

Unbidden, Lalo's scent overwhelmed his memory.

Star Eaters couldn't even smell.

Ro's mind crashed away from the cocoons. For the first time, he *doubted.*

What if Mother Hobi was right? The weight of what he would miss here piled in suddenly, the imagined loneliness, the loss of self. The worthiness of what they did, which he'd not questioned—even for Orro, even for the greater ideal of bringing all civilizations closer, that keykka of cross-knowledge he and other Linguists would contribute to a blossoming future . . .

Fear. That the adventure he envisioned would rust into pointlessness, somewhere far away.

Doubt.

They had to be the least Star-Eater-like thoughts that had ever intruded in the cocoon. He worked frantically to soothe his mind, grabbing for those Warren meditative techniques, resigned that this practice session, too, would be a waste. He would fail here, again, at his greatest ambition.

But—did he want it?

Doubt of place. Doubt of identity. Doubt of purpose . . .

In that moment, he jumped.

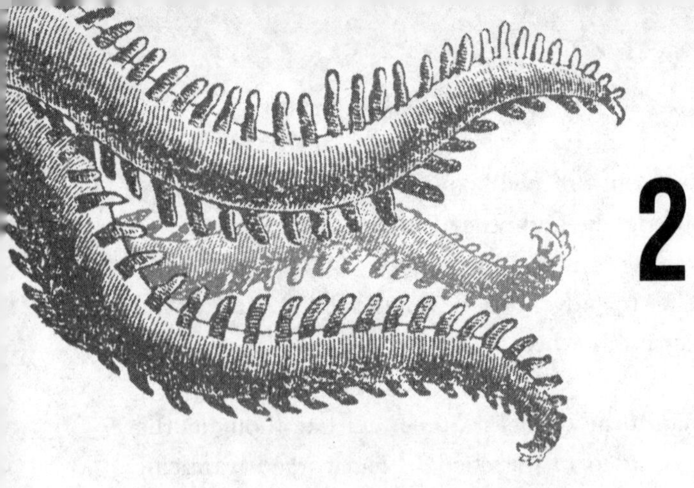

2

The Sound of Space. The Shape of Speech.

The Star Eaters are known to periodically suffer from "confusion periods," a neurological phenomenon unique to their species. These events are marked by memory loss and personality changes, sometimes extreme. Post–confusion period, it is common for a Star Eater's relationships and interactions to differ significantly from prior. They accept these neurological events as a fact of life and they are not disturbed by them, as the Star Eater mind lacks either a strong self-identity or sense of familial connection.

The confusion periods are an unparalleled advantage for remaining undetected. If you discover you have Jumped, you are to immediately mimic such an event and express to those around you that you are lost and confused. It is acceptable to show frustration or upset at your lack of knowledge, but do not attempt to hide it or treat it as abnormal. The Star Eaters do not.

—"Ground Practicalities,"
from the Warren core training opus

Disorienting did not begin to describe Ro's first moments in a new body.

His initial reflexive assumption was that something had gone wrong with the cocoons. New senses heaped across him, *foreign* senses, overwhelming. The astral pocket must have twisted, corrupted, invaded his aura with static and noise and emptiness and chaos—

He went still, desperate for it to pass.

It didn't pass.

It didn't change, either.

Gradually, he adjusted enough for the static to lessen, or to feel as if it did. But still so wrong, because this wasn't the way the practice setups were supposed to go . . .

Maybe the scenario had been reset? While he was inside? The tangle around him began to process into sensation. He could see, *sort of*, though prismed with impossible colors that didn't blend together, and from every direction at once. He could feel, *sort of*, in a full-body explosive prickling that both froze and burned in sensory overload. He could hear, *sort of*, though in more of an echo and mixed with an awareness of vast distances. Vibrations pulsed through every fiber of him. His body was coming apart, splaying to pieces, without pain but so very *wrong*—

Among his surroundings, he became aware first of language.

Someone was talking to him. A Star Eater.

Even without being able to process fully, his mind printed meaning without intervening thought.

ALL RIGHT? It boomed at him, incisive, so much more vivid than ever before.

ALL RIGHT, he answered without thinking. UNBOTHERED.

His own words, too, came unbearably loud. Was he shouting? Gestural languages could shout (so his mind reminded himself, ridiculously—as if running to facts to hide). But this was more like the whole world had multiplied into cacophony in every dimension. A loudness without sound.

WHAT'S HAPPENING? he said.

YOU STOPPED, the other Star Eater answered. *Stopped* here had a graveness imbued. It could have meant "ceased" or "fell" or even "died." CONTINUE? WE ARE OFF QUOTA.

Ro could not parse the question. It might have been *Can you continue?* or *Shall we continue?* or *Will you give permission for us to continue?* The Star Eater language could be light on parts of speech within assumed contexts.

His mental pathways seemed to be stuck on the grammar as a prerequisite, and did not for several moments realize that the larger question was the direct object: *Continue what?*

Was he supposed to know? The practice programs were not usually complex.

Nor was it the same session. The jeweled depth of the starfield was gone. Ro and the other Star Eater were in . . . somewhere metallic, and clunky? He tried to tease out the sensory feedback.

Metallic, and clunky, and dirty. A metal-gridded room, with bars that crisscrossed into the distant beyond. No gravity—a vessel of some kind. Ro wasn't sure how he could tell, but the atmosphere lay gritty, unpleasant and suffocating. Star Eaters didn't breathe, but he could feel the sense organs all up and down his appendages blinking hard in discomfort, curdling away from the environment like a cough.

This body wasn't the same as what the simulation had been a minute ago, either. Smaller than the one the cocoon had originally constructed for him. Stunted in places, with thicknesses and tensions, kinks and pains. The other Star Eater was different, too, less rich floral bloom and more sinewy strands, like a stringy knot.

At least Ro didn't feel like he was coming apart anymore. The sensations were beginning to have a disturbing groundedness to them. As if the session had been changed to make them more real.

His mind ground to a halt.

Real.

Real.

An upgrade to the cocoons couldn't change an astral pocket he'd already started. He would've known that, if he'd thought about it.

His strange new perceptions groped around at the room, himself, the other Star Eater.

ALL RIGHT? the other said again.

If Ro were still Ponto, all four of his stomachs would have flipped over.

WHO AM I? he asked.

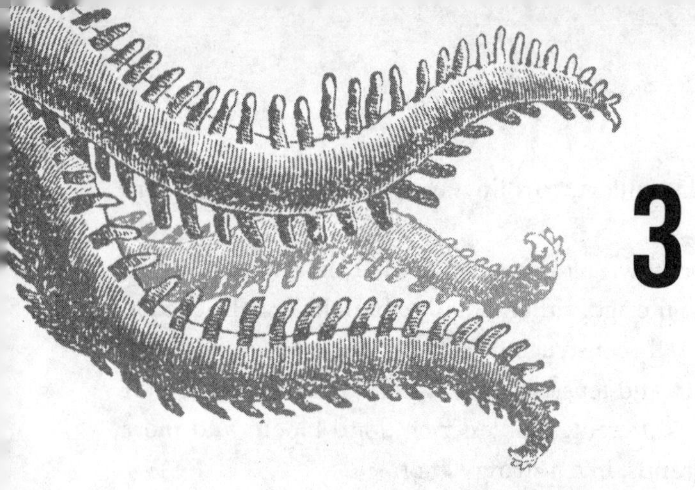

3

Language Unpaired, Senses Unpaired, Life Unpaired

NSL: See, see, you lot are as bad as Dissolution Era! The conglomerate MUST grant them DIGNITY! Saying we've all reformed in our treatment of them but being unwilling to grant the smallest respect—

CIC: You mean your brand of respect.

NSL: I mean BASIC respect. The very name "Star Eater" came out of a petty namecall that got copied everywhere. We claim they're not in servitude any longer but we don't give them names and we smack on labels of a dimorphic gender they don't want—

CIC: Basic respect doesn't mean forcing our version of social norms. It means asking them. They don't give themselves names. They ask for no alternative to "Star Eater" for their species. They do not care that gendered societies often categorize them incorrectly. They have told us this, repeatedly. By all appearances they are of one mind on it.

NSL: How we treat them still matters! We might claim otherwise, but every body politic in this conglomerate only wants them for what they can do for us. We talk big but then rob them of any dignity.

CIC: Not listening to their clearly stated views is what robs them of dignity. Why don't you have a Star Eater member here arguing these points?

NSL: That's a ridiculous question and you know it.

—debate at the Summit for Modern Egalitarianism, between representatives of No Species Less and the Center for Interdomain Communication

---

Shapes descended around Ro—the trailing silhouettes of other workers, the dim shine of astral orbs, the long clanks of sinuous shadow that were the Overseers. Ro tried to ask questions, but any offered answers kept falling out of him, his mind derailing to *I jumped . . . I jumped. I jumped?*

I did it?

I DID IT!

For every minute he spent giddy with accomplishment, he spent the next convinced he must be dreaming or imagining.

No. I think I jumped. I think I did . . . ?

Language surrounded him, undulating gestures from the floating shapes of other Star Eaters or flashes out of the yawning maw-like heads of the Overseers. Ro quailed for a few moments as several of the latter reared close, even as the meaning of the light patterns registered. The Overseers had been designed back in the throes of ugly history: enormous, segmented snakes that could twine through the open bars of the mining ships, exposed to the vacuum.

Twine through, and suppress. It had been easier not to

redesign them, in the centuries since their list of functions stopped including *guard.*

Ro couldn't help wincing away, as if the gaping pits of their heads were diving forth to devour. Was that how Star Eaters saw them? Was the intrinsic flinch a base reflex of the alien body, or his own?

Meaning filtered in to him from all directions. He scrambled to process. He discovered that like most Star Eaters, he was meant to be ore processing—with the brief spark of gladness *That'll be good for Orro*—and that this collector had the designation of mining ship 79. Part of his mind remembered that there were ninety-eight mining ships. (The entire Star Eater population lived in the conglomerate mining fleet. Because where else would they go?)

One of the Overseers flashed at him in increasing aggression about retreating to the cells to rest. Ro realized belatedly it was an order.

WHERE ARE THE CELLS . . . ? he asked. He instinctively tried to smooth his aura before remembering he didn't have one.

Remember—confusion periods are normal for them. No one will see anything amiss.

The Overseer bridled in what had to be artificial impatience. Unless Ro was imagining such a thing. It turned its enormous, spiking maw to the sinewy Star Eater Ro had appeared near, and an instruction flickered out to accompany him and then pair with him for the upcoming shifts.

The next few minutes were nothing but clumsy confusion as Ro tried to learn to use the attraction bands embedded among his cilia. Wearable technology was rare on

Orro thanks to the moon's low resource ceilings, and the cocoons hadn't featured them as part of any scenario. The other Star Eater had to instruct Ro how to skim toward one bar or another in the grid, but he smashed himself against them twice even before they'd left the ore center.

Had this been in the training core somewhere? He didn't remember it!

The Overseer had retreated, thankfully, but some of the astral orbs hovered at a short distance, glowing spheres of pulsing light that made Ro self-conscious. Were they watching him? Did one of them hold the astral fold that connected to Orro, his Seniors' eyes on him already from half a galaxy away? He had to figure out which connected to home. But right now the other Star Eater was trying to patiently guide him out into a channel through the grid—one with enough surrounding struts to vaguely pass for a barred corridor—and he needed all his concentration not to crash again. They edged out of the more open ore center and into the metal trellis of the collector ship, leaving any faraway eyes behind.

The lack of up or down, of any walls or floors to provide reference or boundary to their movement . . . A queasiness welled up in Ro. Or some feeling that mapped to queasiness. He tried to reach his new senses beyond the massive layers of barred framework toward more open space, but they must have been too deep within the ship's bowels. The populated part of each collector was, in these times, a small nucleus of its full size, with the rest a relic stretching many times beyond its present-day uses.

Ro wasn't prepared for the grid to unfold into an abrupt change in structure: a vast bank of identical cubes, each with five solid sides and the sixth side open, and stacked tight against each other ahead and across. It gave him an immediate sense of vertigo, like towered cubicle housing he'd seen images of in realms that weren't Orro . . . even though it marched along the dimension he'd been vaguely thinking of as the floor. His mind flipped, imbuing a cavernous height against a contrast of cramped and unprivate squares.

TAKE ANY VACANT BAY, his companion said. EACH HAS A SHIP-BASED NEXUS POINT. MAKE CERTAIN TO ACTIVATE THE ENCLOSURE FIELD BEFORE REST. THAT IS OBVIOUS, BUT SOME ONES FORGET AND WE FIND THEM FLOATING IN THE ORE PROCESSOR. OR WE DON'T!

Ro wasn't sure if that was supposed to be a joke. None of his lessons had mentioned Star Eater humor. He would have remembered that.

THESE ARE THE CELLS? he asked.

YOU ARE SURPRISED?

NO. YES. I DON'T REMEMBER, Ro stuttered.

He wasn't sure what he'd expected. Didn't the conglomerate repeat over and over that the Star Eaters were not in any forced position any longer; they had full rights; they were free to leave . . . ? The cells were nothing but boxed sameness, mass-produced cavities devoid of any joy or personality, like a zero-gravity barracks.

Or a prison.

Every description of the harshly gridded structure of the mining ships explained it was for practical reasons. After all, neither the Star Eaters nor their work required atmosphere. The conglomerate had long ago agreed that no government should have easier access than another to the vast collectors—a part of the initial détente when none trusted another—hence maintaining a presence via Overseers and astral orbs. There had never been a functional reason for floors.

Ro also knew, intellectually, that the idea of equating *bars* to traps or cages was a cultural construct. One more common to places with lower technology ceilings, like Orro, and entirely absent from societies that lacked a punitive perspective.

Now that he was here, though . . .

He floated awkwardly against one of the colorless bays.

His companion had mentioned nexus points. Maybe the Star Eaters spent all their time in astral nexus pockets, swimming in constructed realities from far away. Or maybe they did nothing for stimulation, and this dull grayness was what they preferred.

Maybe it's what we *prefer,* he corrected himself. *Work is life; work is work . . .*

An acrid wetness had started somewhere among his many parts, one that tasted of dismay and panic.

The other Star Eater still hovered. HOW MUCH DO YOU REMEMBER?

Ro scrambled for an answer. I DON'T KNOW. NOT MUCH. IT'S STRANGE.

He immediately chastised himself. It wasn't strange, not to them, everyone said—

IT IS STRANGE. I HAD ONE ONLY TWO TURNS AGO, the other said. IT'S UNPLEASANT. BUG LUNCH.

Bug lunch? That wasn't a Star Eater phrase—Ro's mind bounced before realizing it was the literal translation of popular nexus slang, a term that had originally come out of Gaxpigs or Lower Senti. Star Eater speech was known to assimilate loanwords and calques faster than almost any other language.

Was that what came of being constantly connected, lost in astral folds to elsewhere? He gazed across the bank of cells. A few did glow with the muted brightness of an astral field, their occupants buried isolated and silent within.

YES, he said. BUG LUNCH.

AT LEAST I REMEMBERED HOW TO USE MY BRACERS, the other Star Eater said. I'LL RETURN NEXT WORK SHIFT. COME FIND ME IF YOU'VE FORGOTTEN HOW TO EXTRUDE YOURSELF!

With that, Ro's guide sashayed away, navigating fluidly among the grid.

He was alone.

A sudden sadness socked into him.

For his hive, for Mother Hobi, and Lalo, and his littersisters and all his kin and everyone, and his compatriots and Seniors at the Warren, and—and his own Ponto body, left breathing but empty in the cocoon, Ro's consciousness forever gone from it. Who would find him? What would they do with the form he'd left behind? It had never seemed important to know before.

Would his hive be told he was dead? Had the Warren gone over this and he missed it?

He could ask. He was to make contact with Orro as quickly as possible. He could ask for news of home.

He'd not been so bad at his studies to have missed memorizing his next instructions. He was to begin by deaddropping reports on the nexus as soon as he arrived, and he had drilled in the directions to a rendezvous point on the collector ship schematics, where Orro's astral orb would find him . . .

The ship stretched forbiddingly in all directions.

It had seemed so much more straightforward in training!

Ro decided to try for the nexus first. Most of the cells lay dark, with neither shadowed movement nor astral glow. He shifted a few spaces down from the corridor and forced himself into one of the uninviting boxes. A ship-based nexus point, his companion had said . . . that meant its connection encompassed the ship, a snapshotted slice that would periodically sync with the galaxy-wide nexus at predetermined intervals.

Meridian paths made real-time nexus connections possible, but most civilizations reserved that for specialized purposes, instead making use of periodic syncs. Realms like Orro, with its lower technology ceiling, did even less—Orro ignored any consistency with the galaxy-wide nexus, instead mostly pulling static libraries and maintaining them for its people.

Ro had assumed, without ever thinking about it, that using a nexus point would be much like using one of the Orro libraries. Except he had no idea what to do. The featureless cell had only one interruption in its surface: an oily circle of some smooth and gelatinous substance in the back wall. No strings or wheels, no indented levers for claws . . .

Had they taught this and he'd forgotten? Had he missed the training?

Ro tentatively pushed an appendage against the slickness. He sank in immediately, as if plunging a piece of himself into a port to elsewhere.

Written information shouted at him from every direction,

in the main Star Eater recorded language of a vibratory shorthand. It shuddered through his membranes until his mind went inside out and sick, like he was falling in a geotherm capsule for too long and too fast, and he flailed and yanked until he slurped the appendage back out again.

That had never happened when reading Star Eater with his Ponto foot.

The attempt left him dizzy, every one of his new senses piling atop each other in brutal conspiracy. Ro gave up and closed out as much of the sensory noise as he could.

Tomorrow. Tomorrow he would contact Orro.

Star Eaters didn't sleep, but they were supposed to be able to enter a resting trance to recover energy. Tomorrow he could . . . or, next shift rather, since the collectors didn't have a concept of day or night . . .

Rest, calm, come back to it. Meditation techniques would come in handy right now, wouldn't they, if you'd paid attention.

He tried some of the basic ones. They lulled him for a brief pulse before his concentration snapped, mind wandering.

How had he jumped? He'd been thinking about—about everything Ponto, and nothing Star Eater. Had the confusion periods themselves seeded the Star Eater language with so many concepts of *doubt*? Perhaps the body he was in had just been entering a true confusion period, or exiting one, with disorientation that so exactly matched Ro's . . . An embarrassing way to succeed; he might leave it out of the report. *A lie of omission.*

Or, in the Star Eater language: simply a lie. Such a harsh bludgeon of a word.

It'll be all right. Have to find my feet. No. No feet, remember.

No feet, no aura, no sense of smell. No breathing, no claws, no gender . . .

That last was more unsettling than he'd expected. The Ponto were a dimorphic species with bimodal gender, but their linguistic constructs didn't map the way many other gendered species' did. Ponto tended to identify with mating role when young, then later via one's position within the hive. Pronouns and adjectives were gender-neutral but titles were not, and most Ponto switched between titles according to life stage.

There were exceptions—but Ro had always assumed that if he were to stay in his home domain he would shift back and forth as most Ponto did, once he hived as an adult and raised young. He had not expected to struggle so much with the sudden lack.

In gendered languages, Star Eaters had historically been assigned female labels. Part of it might have been an outsider categorization that they were "all mothers," since all Star Eaters could, theoretically, reproduce via asexual budding . . .

Theoretically.

One of Ro's most ambitious mission directives was that very question.

The worst-kept secret in the galaxy was that the Star Eaters were dying. So long-lived it had been difficult to catch the scope of the problem, but increasingly urgent treatises had been flung forth by academics, activists, politicians. They all agreed: Every plunge into distant records showed the Star Eaters had long decreased in reproduction until they must have ceased altogether.

One had to go back age upon age to find a confirmed record of a new Star Eater.

No Star Eaters, no meridian element. No meridian, no ability to slide between distant space. All intersystem transportation would disintegrate. And with it . . .

Catastrophe. Far worse than Dissolution. Famine, infrastructure breakdown—whole planets would collapse. Massive civilizations in numbers impossible to move elsewhere, or to support in place without the frequent trade provided by the meridian paths.

Orro would collapse. Its moon relied on imported resources—food, oxygen, hydrogen. Even with long-agreed laws capping power drain, nowhere on the moon was within running distance of self-sufficient.

The Star Eaters were thc only ones who could sense the meridian element in distant space. The only ones who could mine it. They did so naturally, natively. Centuries of outsider scientists had flung themselves against the problem, only to crumble in frustration.

In modern times, the Star Eaters did not seem to hold any animosity toward the conglomerate for past mistreatment and made no attempt to stop other species from questioning or studying them. But they remained enigmatic. None seemed bothered that they had not borne young in an excruciatingly long time. When asked, they would say only that their bodies "*know when it is time.*"

Apparently, it was never time.

And nobody had ever been able to figure out a technology that would replicate what the Star Eaters did.

The galaxy still had a distance of centuries before all the Star Eaters exceeded their lengthy unspooling lifespans, though less before a population decline would cause the pinch of diminished resources. Some voices already loudly panicked about it; some had turned anger at the Star Eaters themselves: *Why can't they just have some babies, why are they so selfish??*

Most continued to ignore such a slow death, trusting that someone, somewhere, would solve it before anything turned too dire.

Worlds couldn't just *die*, after all.

Ro might be a "cheerful disaster." But he'd made it, here, to be Orro's chance. The galaxy's chance.

The stakes towered to infinity. Ro's work here was important for its own sake, but beyond that . . . what he learned could save civilization, septillions of lives.

He'd get it right. He would.

Tomorrow.

Even if he *doubted*, he would never let his people down.

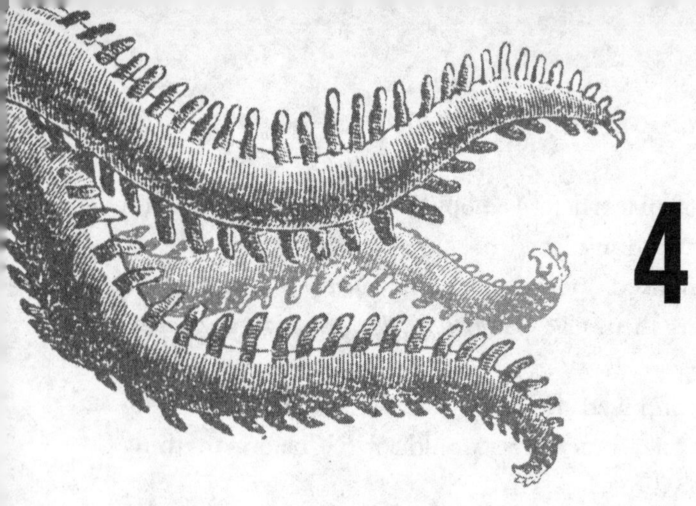

4

Words to Devour, Minds to Remember

The Star Eaters derive pleasure from work. Regarding the speculation as to why they chose to continue in primarily the same quasi-servile role once their citizenship rights were restored: I believe other species overthink this. With their survival needs provided and the pressure of higher decisions removed, they could focus on the mining. This has turned to a compulsion for most, until they wish to do nothing else.

—Poda, Orro Linguist,
Report #012 post-Jump

By the following work shift, Ro had successfully pushed back his melancholy. After all, how could he dwell on such insecurities when he was *here*? Everything he'd dreamed, a whole world and culture he might learn and discover and unlock for the realms of history!

Today—today he would embrace it. Today he would figure everything out, and achieve contact with Orro, and be lauded for his success as he dove into an invigorating new life.

He told himself so enough times to be convincing.

The same ropey Star Eater who'd brought him to the cells came back for him, as promised. The parts of Ro that weren't yet thinking in Star Eater speech automatically assigned her female labeling, as he had been taught. He ignored his own discomfort kicking back—*That's not a Star Eater attitude. They don't care.*

The ends of his guide's sparse fronds curled up like she was happy to see him. WORK IS WORK! SHALL WE?

UNBOTHERED, Ro answered.

They went together to the ore center, already filled with Star Eaters and the occasional Overseer, all drifting purposefully across parts of the cavernous, metal-gridded space and attending to duties Ro couldn't yet parse. The caustic permeation of the place made his body seize and clench, but his senses had begun to register more comprehensibly.

Ro teased out the inputs and poked at them. Vision, vision was easiest—it spread over his body and compounded like beaded glass. He could see his own appendages shaded dark, with the knobby white puckers of scarring in places; and with his guide close by, smaller and sprightly and more marbled . . . the other workers trended from blacks and violets into colors Ro had never seen and could not yet match with a word. Other sensations manifested as sharpnesses and pressures that were harder to describe, with no Ponto analogue—Star Eaters had so many field and force senses, and Ro had no frame of reference—

An Overseer's pitted maw reared out of the dimness,

the bulk of its sinuousness twining out of sight amid the grid. It flashed something at Ro's companion that Ro only caught the edges of—edges that spiked with hostility and aggression.

BASELINE, she answered blithely. WORK IS LIFE.

The Overseer retreated.

ALL RIGHT? Ro asked nervously.

UNBOTHERED, she said, her appendages rippling with no hint of untruth. COME, QUOTA AWAITS! I WILL INSTRUCT!

Ro followed obediently.

He knew it was incorrect, but it didn't take long to start thinking of his companion as You-In-Front. Of course Ro knew "You-In-Front" wasn't *actually* her name. In fact it was also what she had been calling him the whole time. Star Eaters used at least fourteen different ways of referring to each other, with between nine and twenty more contextual inflections of each depending on how one counted . . . all relative ways of saying "you." A far cry from Ponto's measly two. (*Front* wasn't even a good literal translation, as Star Eaters faced in all directions at once and had nothing like the same concept of *front.* But a proximate beneficial-agent second-person vocative was what a Ponto would think of as "the person in front of me," or, in Ponto, "you.")

Ro had always been fascinated with how inflected the Star Eater language was for some words, versus how much grammatical differentiation seemed to have dropped off others. Nobody had worked out the reasons for it. Linguists from many worlds argued over how the language ought to be categorized, given the messiness of its morphemes, and some scholars invented new and narrow morphological typologies just to deal with Star Eater. Ro wondered if the Star Eaters had ever had their own Linguists, once upon a time . . .

You-In-Front herself had a tendency to elide inflectional affixes in places Ro hadn't learned, dropping tense and case wholesale to the point where he worried that his own speech might seem too precise. Fortunately she hadn't seemed to notice yet.

DO YOU FEEL IT?

Ro belatedly realized he'd lost track of her instructions.

I DISAPPOINT, he said, one of several phrases that mapped to an *I'm sorry* in Ponto. FEEL WHAT?

MERIDIAN! You-In-Front answered. RELAX. TRY AGAIN. I MUST CONNECT YOU.

The Star Eaters' meridian ability operated on genetic memory, but the instinct wouldn't spring to life automatically like Ro's new senses. Their species didn't have anything like a Ponto empathic sense with each other, but they had a sort of . . . connective ability, a melding and guidance of instinct.

Ro readied himself, expecting it to happen with no fuss. At least now that he was paying attention.

It didn't. Ro tried, and coughed—sort of, it felt like coughing—and tried again, while his new senses stabbed pokier and pointier. You-In-Front stayed breezy and encouraging, but frustration began creeping up on Ro and tensing him out of the attempt—

He wasn't helped by those chaotic Star Eater senses, wrapping in every three-hundred-sixty-degree slice and so loud and constant and hard to shut out. Not *literally* loud; the vacuum of space had no sound. But Ro's mind assigned metaphor and description to the distractions and vibrations, and they caught him in a thousand directions at once: grinding machinery across several separate diagonals, and groups of workers swinging along invisible paths at odds to each other, and the stark, gleaming eyes of the astral orbs winking in and out of the dimness, eyes over every metaphorical shoulder . . .

In the background, that same Overseer still hovered. Was it Ro's imagination, or did it seem to be watching them specifically? Its head drifted out in midair, like some of the aquifer creatures back home who stuck themselves to an underwater rock and let an appendage float to catch food.

Naturally it was hard to concentrate! What had that Overseer been saying earlier? Had it been asking about him?

WE GO AGAIN, You-In-Front said.

I—I DON'T— Ro gasped. He was beginning to feel like warmed-over nut pulp. WHAT IF I CAN'T—

DO NOT WORRY, YOU WILL LIKE THIS! You-In-Front bounced a little. IT IS THE GOOD PART.

It was an odd word for *good*—more like *buoyant* or *pleasantly rounded.* Ro's mind snagged. He had been taught that Star Eaters didn't have a direct analogue for *fun*, as they did not perceive enjoyment in such a way. *They are contented to work*, reported countless studies of the culture. *Satisfaction from routine . . .*

But the phrasing You-In-Front had just used—

He shook it off. *Concentrate, concentrate.* What if he was the first jumper in the history of Orro to make it all this way, and then try and try and never be able to sink into the vital, essential meridian intuition that was *supposed to be his whole role here*—

And suddenly, he could.

Like an optical illusion that leapt out of the background. Shining highlights spilling in veins through the open space, pattering through in an avalanche of opening blossoms, springing up so strong and bright and sharp that Ro could have sworn it *sang.*

Meridian.

It would have stolen his breath if he had any.

I CAN FEEL IT! he cried. IT'S THERE, HOW DO I KNOW IT'S THERE?

You-In-Front shivered in humor. I TOLD YOU! THE GOOD PART. YOU CAN SPOT FIRST THEN!

Spotting! Right—Ro knew what that meant—Star Eaters worked in pairs or groups, with one acting as a "spotter." Ro tried to recall the information, but he needed a moment to process this because the panorama was still growing and brilliant and *beautiful*—

I WILL MINE. YOU SAY WHERE, You-In-Front said.

Mining. Star Eater bodies collected the meridian element in microscopic spindles as they fed—in nature, this buildup over centuries would allow an entire Star Eater cluster to blink across stellar distances to a new nebular feeding ground, whenever the nutrients they absorbed from the cosmic dust ran low. It had always sounded grand and glorious to Ro, whorling across the cosmos between clouds of stardust.

Optimized mining was far less so. The collector ships

came to where the Star Eaters sensed high concentrations of meridian, then trawled the area shift after shift, navigating to aim at the densest pockets. A spotter for each worker group would direct the others in pushing themselves through the hotspots to the point of engorgement. The spindles could then be extracted off their bodies, processed, and adhered to any variety of technology to form bubbles of interstellar travel and communication.

Which all sounded much less enchanting.

Still, Ro couldn't prevent his cilia from trilling in excitement and nerves. Every new sensation was a discovery, a revelation—

—one that morphed almost instantly to panic. REDWARD! he tried to shout to You-In-Front. NO, BLUEWARD—NO—

Why was he so clumsy? Why couldn't he—? He'd studied Star Eater directionality; he'd studied it extensively! They had no up and down or left and right but instead used words that seemed to have a bizarre lack of etymological connection—but Ro had drilled, and trained, and drilled, to make it automatic rather than a translation he had to operate in his head every time—but now that he was here and under pressure—

Was that Overseer riveted on him right now?

STRIKE THAT! he flailed. GO IN THE—IN THE DIRECTION—

His appendages thrashed, he lost track of watching the other sides of him, and he whipped smack into the path of another worker.

Both pinwheeled. Ro pawed at his bracers, trying to arrest himself, and pulled up at an entirely different angle than he'd started at. The Star Eater he'd collided with had careened into her whole worker group. Ro's horrified new awareness showed spindles of precious meridian sloughing off into space, a heartbreaking light show.

The other worker was much faster than Ro. She'd yanked herself to a halt, and she balled up to arrow straight at him, tight with fury. Ro tried to fall away, but he couldn't figure out how.

I TRANSGRESSED. I TRANSGRESSED! he babbled. Another apology term. I WILL IMPROVE, I TRANSGRESSED!

IT'S CONFUSION, You-In-Front overlapped loyally, defending him. CALM, IT'S ONLY CONFUSION—

CONFUSION IS NO EXCUSE! You-Behind's charge nearly didn't stop, pulling up so fast and close that she loomed in his senses.

An Overseer's head yawned abreast of them out of nowhere. The same one who'd been watching, he was almost sure—but so fast he hadn't even seen it move—

Cease this, it flashed. *Return to duties.*

The effect was instant. You-In-Front and You-Behind both curled away and stilled.

Ro trailed off in the midst of apologizing again. The tension screamed louder than any other sense.

IT WAS MY TRANSGRESSION, he signed timidly to the Overseer. CAN I DO SOMETHING? CAN I FIX IT?

Its head reared as if about to strike. *Return to duties.*

Ro jerked for his bracers, yanking himself away and back toward You-In-Front. You-Behind made one last poisonous gesture in Ro's direction before lurching back toward her worker group, and the Overseer moved away.

The ends of Ro's tentacles trembled in space.

IT WAS THE CONFUSION, You-In-Front said comfortingly. LET'S SWITCH.

Despite himself, Ro noticed that she'd fully inflected the pronoun but dropped conjugation on the action—like *We switch*, but *we* was *you-and-I-two-people-speaker-inclusive-nominative-agency*. He had to adjust his own speech. How was he getting so much wrong? Would she notice? Would anyone notice?

If he made another mistake . . .

I DISAPPOINT, I DISAPPOINT, he stammered to You-In-Front. WILL THERE BE TROUBLE?

NO TROUBLE, she said, surprisingly calm. THE ONLY TROUBLE IS FOR MISSING QUOTA.

WHAT IF I CAN'T MEET QUOTA?

She paused as if he'd said something strange. WHY WOULD YOU NOT MEET QUOTA? WORK IS LIFE.

WORK IS WORK, Ro said. BUT CONFUSION . . .

CONFUSION DOES NOT INTERFERE WITH QUOTA.

He *had* said something strange. But what? Ro was missing something, something he shouldn't; he was going to give himself away . . .

TRUE! he agreed, a beat too late.

He wished desperately that Star Eater had more discourse markers, fillers like *oh* or *well* or *I see* that he could use to bridge space. Fluidity in discourse markers always gave him more confidence. They were notoriously hard for secondary speakers, but Ro had a knack, and sounding native on the in-betweens made him *feel* fluent. But Star Eater was remarkably sparse.

Stop getting distracted, he ordered himself. *Focus!*

To his relief, mining was easier than spotting. He turned out to be barely better at following Star Eater directional words than he was at choosing them—but You-In-Front gave off other cues that oriented him, plus he could feel the meridian element himself. He wondered at first why they had spotters at all; why not simply have the Star Eaters move through on their own and let the spindles cling on like a hitchhiker moss? But he hadn't counted on how disorienting the mining process would be. Ro would have sworn he couldn't feel it happening, but by halfway through the remainder of the shift, his movements had grown loaded and dizzy.

The whole time, his dispersed sensory organs were hyperaware of the Overseer lurking off to one side, its mouth still weaving in their direction.

What if it's marked me as acting different? What can it do?

The Warren training had mostly emphasized the importance of obeying the Overseers' empowered discipline, that all Star Eaters did, and one mustn't stand out, mustn't draw attention . . .

TIME TO EXTRACT, You-In-Front said, pulling his attention back. SEE? NOT HARD.

NOT HARD, Ro echoed. Though he wasn't sure he agreed. Not difficult, but tiring, and uncomfortable, and stressful, to do day after day after day. *Work is life* . . .

WHEN YOU ARE SPOTTER, REMIND YOUR WORKERS TO EXTRACT, You-In-Front advised. MORE OFTEN IS BETTER THAN LESS.

BECAUSE OF THE INSTABILITY, Ro remembered, trying to keep up. His limbs slogged, reluctant to form precise words. He'd been taught how once the meridian element left its own dimension, large quantities could prove unpredictable. Massive resources and development went into proper meridian storage.

NO, NOT AT ALL! IF YOU COULD DRAW ENOUGH MERIDIAN IN A SHIFT TO TRIGGER IT, YOU WOULD BE AN IDOL, You-In-Front said. She might have been laughing at him. YOU GET SLOW. THAT IS WHY.

She was right about that. Ro's thoughts sagged as heavy as his body. Like a bloating in all four stomachs after an Orro feast day, but everywhere . . . Intellectually, he knew a side effect of the mining was that the Star Eaters were constantly over-absorbing nutrients. At least he would never go hungry.

He mustered up a sign of acknowledgment to You-In-Front and stopped trying to speak.

Extraction involved passing through a tunnel-like machine that felt like a full Ponto undercoat exfoliation, sucking every plug of dirt and dust out of the pores Star Eaters didn't have. The sudden lightening was a shock to the system—but Ro wilted in dismay when a light pattern flashed the measured output.

SO LITTLE? he said.

You-In-Front waved him off. AS LONG AS YOU'RE MEETING QUOTA.

HOW MUCH IS QUOTA?

Her appendages stirred in consternation, as if she didn't understand the question. WORK IS LIFE.

Again with the word *quota*. What was he missing?!

WORK IS LIFE, Ro agreed quickly. WE WILL MEET QUOTA. He imitated her earlier grammatical elision by making it *We meet quota*, and she seemed satisfied.

Ro wished he could ask for a rest. How much of the shift was left? Other groups of workers had been moving seamlessly together with no pause, up to six or ten sometimes, maximizing collection in a way Ro couldn't yet fathom. His own mind and body were drained after his first try. He had to get more efficient.

Especially because . . . if he didn't . . .

He and You-In-Front had moved all the way across the processing center from that one Overseer, but Ro could feel its mechanical gaze following.

It was only hitting him now how *alone* he was here. Out on the crumbling edge, with no one to lean on, no one to help.

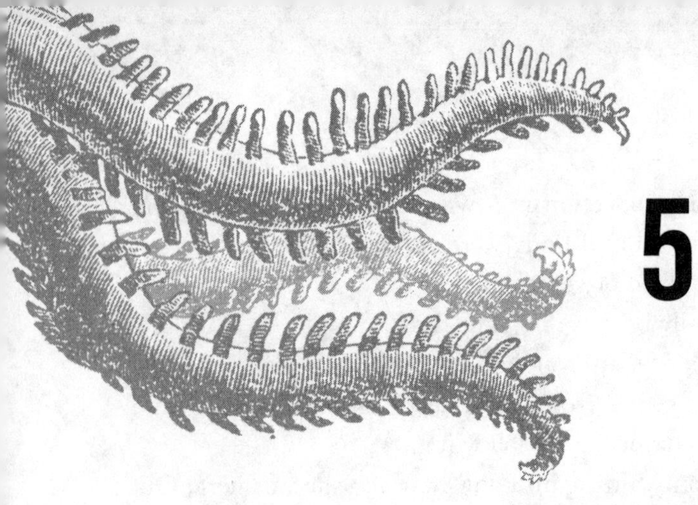

5

Navigating an Infinite World Is Statistically Impossible

We shall never wash ourselves free of the blood of those we call the Star Eaters. It soaks every meridian path in the galaxy.

—Chumche Pany, high priest of the Sewaw Order

The Star Eaters have chosen to continue mining operations for the good of the conglomerate. We're not doing anything wrong.

—Drî Flim, Chair of the Ter Thosh Elected Council, in a comment for the Hūskwasōng news organization

We left them with nothing, then we wonder why they stayed.

—Tomyo, Accordance Age philosopher

Ro had nearly convinced himself that the Overseer stalking his movements would follow him straight out of the ore center. But once he had finished his shift and escaped, he found himself spinning alone in the grid. He dragged himself back along the same route to the same cell.

Only to find a Star Eater hovering outside it.

He thought he recognized her stumpy ombre and puffy cilia as having been in a cell near his. She retreated slightly on his approach, and Ro tried not to react.

Was she watching him, too?

You're paranoid, he told himself. *You're paranoid, and you're overreacting. Work on following your instructions to reach Orro.*

Despite his exhaustion, he tried to pace out some distance of exploration from the cells. But he still had no idea how the schematics he'd studied mapped against the disconcerting repetition of the three-dimensional ship. Some of the astral orbs hovered from a distance, appearing and disappearing out of the dimness, but Ro had no way of knowing which Orro watched from—or even which ones had watchers at all.

Ever since the Star Eaters had been granted conglomerate membership, the collectors had no surveillance by law—nothing beyond the Overseers, which were limited-function automata, and the orbs, which contained astral folds connecting to each member of the conglomerate. Each domain was permitted one astral orb per ship, to protect their interests or to inquire after the miners, and a government could watch from them in real time if desired. These days, many were largely left empty, since real-time meridian connections consumed such high resources. But some wealthier realms preferred to keep watch, or to send parades of researchers or scientists to speak to the workers.

Those same governments jealously audited each other to ensure none of their competitors was engaging in illegal monitoring of the meridian trade. Supposedly, that meant Ro should safely know when someone might be watching.

It didn't make him any less tense.

Venturing far enough to leave the cells behind was even more nerve-racking. Ro had to stay meticulous about wrong turns. Barred lines stacked in shadows in every direction, crisscrossing at alien angles—threatening to swallow him in their sameness, every corner repeating identical.

Like the Star Eaters were said to be. As consistent in opinion as a culture could be without being part of a hive mind.

(Although, the Jah-Minn *were* a hive mind and still had more individuation. The larger Jah-Minn "minds" frequently separated into sects, and several had suffered civil wars. Two Jah-Minn minds had emigrated to other domains and successfully attained individual citizenship for each of their hundreds of thousands of members.)

Maybe Orro would guide Ro in pushing the edges of that famed Star Eater constancy. A comfortable majority of cultures valued conformity over individuality—scholars had long explored such mores, from the loner society in Bash Tso to the adherence camps of Corimonte, or the educational system of Faragall that placed newness over knowledge versus the Khord Confederation who did the extreme opposite. But even the most consistent of peoples usually had their exceptions.

Not so for the Star Eaters. Or so people said. Would personalities as different as You-In-Front and You-Behind truly always be of the same mind?

Ro was so unused to having regular nexus access that it took him half an off-shift of frustrated hiking to realize he could likely pull up augmented filters with maps of the ship. He had to figure out the nexus access anyway and start dropping reports—Orro would still wish to speak to him directly, but at least he could begin his important cultural work.

He stumped back to the cells. The same lurking Star Eater waited, right outside the cell he'd been using.

He tried to ignore her.

He ducked into the cell and poked at the nexus point again. An identical sensory chaos clamored. How was it possibly usable that way! He considered venturing back out, but one peek showed his neighbor still hanging in space outside, just—there.

Waiting.

Ro decided to rest instead.

When You-In-Front came to get him for their next shift, the lurker had disappeared, doubtless to her own work shift. But some sort of commotion drew Ro's attention from down the cell block—Overseers, five or six of them, their sinuous bodies overlapping in swirling movement like aquifer eels.

Ro hadn't seen them around the workers' rest quarters like this. And in their midst, a Star Eater, one he didn't recognize . . . mottled patterns across thready, curling appendages that stretched from each other in lacy fans.

WHAT IS IT? WHAT IS HAPPENING? Ro inquired of You-In-Front.

NOT OF US, she answered, nonchalant. NO CONCERN.

She moved toward the steady stream of Star Eaters ambling toward the ore center. Ro lagged after. None of the other workers seemed particularly engaged with what the Overseers were doing, either . . .

Except Ro's lurker, just alighting at the cell bank. Ro

couldn't figure out how he knew what she paid attention to, but something in the arc of her drift, spooled as it was around an awareness of the still-unfolding incident . . . she was as invested as Ro.

COME, You-In-Front hurried Ro along. WORK IS LIFE!

But even as he followed, Ro's panoramic senses allowed him to watch until the overlapping grid hid what lay behind. Allowed him to see as Overseers escorted the Star Eater in their midst away into the darkness. She seemed to go silently, willingly, limbs spread slack, untouched by her ominous chaperones.

Ro was prevented from dwelling by his work shift, which desiccated him with fatigue enough to drive out every other thought. Once he made it back to the cells again—membranes aching, his paranoia in a new spin about the Overseer watching him the whole time *again*—the commotion was long gone, along with its unlucky charge.

But the same stumpy, faded Star Eater waited by his cell. Squatting in the same place.

Ro regarded her for a moment, unsettled. Could a Star Eater be said to stare when they could see in all directions? What defined staring for them? *Why would she stare?*

He had the overwhelming urge to break the tension. In training they'd been warned of the Star Eaters' cultural reticence—*Far less likely to start up casual conversations than you will be*, they'd been told. *Beware of overly friendly overtures. Do not engage in small talk.* Orro was on the highest end of outgoing friendliness toward strangers; the Star Eaters among the lowest.

But so much here was leaving him tired and frayed and

swimming against a thousand unknowns—and across history, almost nothing had been solved by *not* using language, had it?

Ro swept up to her before he could rethink.

WILL YOU HELP ME? His insides popped, but he managed to keep the motions relaxed. Mostly. I CAN'T REMEMBER HOW TO USE THE NEXUS . . .

She started, a brief contraction like she was surprised to be addressed. YOU CAN'T REMEMBER?

THE CONFUSION, he explained. I JUST HAD ONE.

THE CONFUSION, she repeated, as though digesting it. I JUST HAD ONE.

A pause stretched between them.

THAT'S WHY I CAN'T REMEMBER, Ro said. BECAUSE OF THE CONFUSION.

YES. THAT'S WHY I CAN'T REMEMBER, You-Outside said.

Ro's disorientation began to morph into a minor panic. He should never have started this conversation.

Then it hit him—in half the interaction, they'd both dropped subjects and inflections. He thought he'd done it in a way that made sense—the Star Eater language was supposed to do it all the time; You-In-Front had been doing it all the time. But a native would do it in a way that would scan correctly . . .

To You-Outside, *could the entire conversation have been reversed*?

Was Ro that bad at this?

YOU JUST HAD A CONFUSION PERIOD, he said cautiously, fully declining and conjugating everything so there could be no misunderstanding.

She pulled away slightly. Maybe irritably—Ro was beginning to believe the Star Eater lexicon had much more semantic nuance than he'd been taught.

I TOLD YOU I HAD A CONFUSION PERIOD, You-Outside said. She continued to drop the pronouns and most of the grammar: *Told—confusion period.*

Ro took that as confirmation. Along with a good helping of relief—confusion could explain any of her odd behavior. He threw out a sign of acknowledgment and went to move past her.

Then paused.

She looked . . . lonely.

ALL RIGHT? Ro asked.

UNBOTHERED. BASELINE.

I JUST HAD A CONFUSION PERIOD TOO, he said, again fully inflecting it.

You-Outside reacted then, opening toward him like an unfurling punctuation mark. Ro guessed that she finally understood. Sympathy and anxiety chased through him in alternating measures. He wondered if he should have left it . . . One strange interaction might have been forgettable for her, but now that she knew he'd made an error common to secondary speakers—

How would she suspect, though? The rest of the conglomerate doesn't know Orro can do this. She won't assume you're a Ponto-in-another-body, nobody would, not the Overseer who keeps watching you either—you just have to make sure nobody has any other sorts of misgivings—

THAT'S WHY I ASKED HELP WITH THE NEXUS, he said hurriedly. IF YOU'RE WILLING.

YOU FORGOT THE NEXUS? You-Outside said.

YOU DIDN'T? Ro blurted. *Confusion periods are different for everyone. It's not suspicious. It's not.*

You-Outside took deliberate time in answering again, then said, I WILL SHOW YOU.

They went together to one of the nexus points. The cell was small for both of them, and Ro pressed himself against its walls to give her space—Star Eater culture considered physical over-closeness to be vastly impolite.

THE SHIP HAS MANY LIBRARIES, You-Outside explained. She reached out with delicacy, as if about to make a fine brushstroke on the nexus point. YOU CAN PULL ANY. IF YOU WISH A LIBRARY FROM ELSEWHERE, OR ONE NEWLY RELEASED, YOU MUST REQUEST AND WAIT.

Wait for the next sync, when the ship made a meridian connection with a station. Ro had mostly known that.

You-Outside trailed the ends of her cilia just along the surface of the connective port, drawing out a bead of material. AN ASTRAL LIBRARY. YOUR THOUGHTS WILL GUIDE.

IT HAS A MENTAL COMPONENT? Ro asked.

OF COURSE. HOW ELSE?

Ro was used to Ponto technology interfacing mentally, but other species didn't have an empathic sense. It hadn't occurred to him that other worlds could work the same way.

But then, Star Eaters activated their genetic memory through some type of mental link, and perceiving meridian worked that way, too, and—he remembered asking, once, whether in their studies they should fear jumping into a non–Star Eater by accident. He'd been told no, as the Star Eater jumps were rare even after concerted effort, and jumping to a species with no mental aptitude at all was even more difficult. *Possible*, his instructors had said, because the Ponto empathic sense was what made it work in the first place, but vanishingly unlikely.

Still, he vaguely remembered now that many other species used mental nexus interfaces. Maybe every mind gave off something, even if you couldn't feel it.

The bead You-Outside had pulled from the interface had hardened at once, and she showed him how to insert it into a bracer. CRACK TO ACTIVATE. YOUR THOUGHTS WILL GUIDE, she repeated. IT WILL MIX FROM THE LIBRARY. IF YOU WANT EXACT, YOU MUST SET IT.

Ro had only wanted to search and read, not create a whole artificial environment blended out of a thousand information pools. But if he asked about something that basic, You-Outside might think him dimmer than she already did. Some civilizations started an astral field for even the simplest nexus interaction—maybe if he wanted to do any research, he had to imagine up an artificial librarian first.

THIS WILL MAKE AN ASTRAL POCKET? he confirmed.

She quivered an acknowledgment. WE COULD SHARE ONE, IF YOU WANT. WHERE DO YOU WISH TO GO?

Ro couldn't have said why, but her tentative, half-bloomed posture put him in mind of his younger littersisters—all timid shyness, as if waiting for his approval.

YOU CHOOSE, he said.

You-Outside drew a bead into her own bracer and cracked it.

Predictably, she cast them into a swirling nebula, clouds of color blossoming against the purest dark of space. The Star Eater native habitat.

Ro wasn't surprised by the choice. What he hadn't guessed was how it would stun him.

Compared to what the Orro cocoons could raise . . . the detail and immersion thrilled him to every tip. Or perhaps it was his Star Eater senses, engaged in every way by a simulation made to hook them, field particles inundating from all sides. Unlike in the Orro cocoons, his and You-Outside's bodies were their own, the astral field filtering out only their surroundings.

IT'S BEAUTIFUL, Ro whispered, his motions the barest stir.

YES, answered You-Outside. But her appendages drifted limp, like she didn't want to be there anymore.

Or wanted too much to be there?

WHAT ABOUT A VISIT? Ro probed.

YES. She waved at their surroundings. A VISIT.

NOT LIKE THIS. IN REAL LIFE.

You-Outside was blank. Unreadable. FOR WHAT REASON?

Ro tried to think what he would say to Coro or Sa when they were embarrassed to open up or didn't think he would understand. SOMETIMES A THING NEEDS NO REASON?

She twitched. UNBOTHERED. WORK IS WORK.

Ro crashed back to where he was—the secrets, the danger, *What are you doing, trying to be a hive sibling? You're supposed to be a Star Eater!*

WORK IS LIFE, he said hastily. UNBOTHERED. BASELINE. I WOULD NOT LIKE TO BE TAKEN, LIKE THE ONE LAST SHIFT. He was talking too much now, anxieties bubbling out of him. But she'd been watching what happened earlier, he knew she had. She'd had questions, too; maybe she'd asked—

TAKEN? echoed You-Outside.

THE OVERSEERS, Ro said. THEY TOOK ONE LIKE US. BEFORE MY SHIFT.

NOT TOOK. WENT, You-Outside corrected. THEY DO NOT TAKE. THAT ONE WENT.

FOR WHAT REASON? Ro asked.

FOR CORRECTION.

A tremor crinkled through Ro out to his ends. He tried to mask it. CORRECTION OF WHAT?

INSUFFICIENCIES. You-Outside's motions were neutral. WORK IS LIFE.

Ro scraped at his memory. Had prior reports to Orro mentioned *correction*? Perhaps it was rare, or minor, or both. Perhaps he would see the absent Star Eater tumble in next shift, ready to work.

If I am "insufficient"—will the Overseers collect me? Is being Star Eater synonymous with a perfect willingness to disappear?

He didn't dare press more. He had a sudden urge to flee this conversation before You-Outside saw any more of his own *insufficiencies*, before she called the Overseers, before they instructed him into a compliance that he couldn't refuse without revealing himself.

But before he could, You-Outside moved as if to ask something in return. HAVE THEY TOLD YOU . . . She hitched and curled into herself for a beat. I WISH TO DO WELL. HAVE THEY TOLD YOU HOW MUCH IS QUOTA?

Ro froze.

How had You-In-Front answered? WORK IS LIFE! he cried, much too fast.

WORK IS LIFE, she agreed. WHAT IS THE QUOTA? I WISH TO MEET QUOTA.

WORK IS WORK, Ro said. Sagely. Desperately. As if any of it made sense.

Only after he had finally escaped and hurried off in a random direction did it occur to him that he'd handled that all wrong.

If You-Outside remembered the definition of "quota" the same way he did, then he *hadn't* messed up the word. Which meant it must be a recent linguistic drift, which meant *What is quota* was a perfectly normal question—

And he'd tripped up, again, by panicking and pretending it wasn't.

I don't know, he should have said. *I asked, but the answer was confusing.* That would have been the response of someone who had nothing to hide.

Everything had seemed so simple from Orro: Learn the language perfectly, and everything would follow. If Ro had paid more attention—if he hadn't skipped so much of the non-linguistic training—would it have prevented this constant drowning that threatened to close over his head with each misstep?

What would he do if the Overseers came for him? What *should* he do if—

Ro's internal recriminations cut off suddenly. He had been racing away from the cells without paying attention, and . . .

He had no idea where he was.

He spun in a slow circle, a sick fear clambering up every fiber of him in a silent scream. The grid climbed into the endless distance through every sensory organ on every side. Ro had lost which direction he'd come from. Neither his coruscating vision—nor any of those new visceral sensations of depth—gave him sign or feature that could help.

Only the ship's grid, laddering away forever.

No up. No down. No backward or forward.

No visible nexus points. Which, he remembered too late, he could have pulled ship's maps from—maps that would keep him from wandering without end, haunting the bowels of a too-large, too-empty collector ship. Like the pitch-dark maze of a deserted tunnel system: all mooring gone and sentenced to an everlasting tomb.

Oh, no.

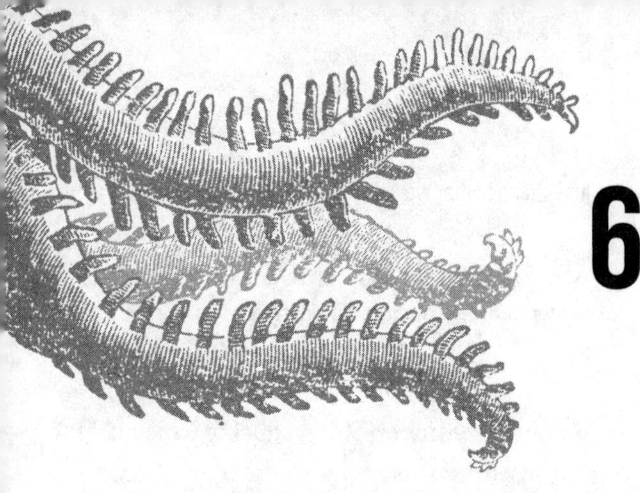

6

The Truths We Believe, the Truths We Agree On

People have yelled all up and down and round 'bout how we ought to reform the Overseer system. Anyone invested in Star Eater conditions starts off pretty boiled about it, like why do we have this brutal holdover from Dissolution in charge of 'em? But then if those same folks try, they run right up against the practical side, every time.

Not talking will or resources, either. The top problem is nobody knows what to reform 'em into.

There's gotta be some means of keeping the mining ships on track, right? And the Star Eaters, well, they don't wanna do it themselves and probably can't anyway. So you get most redesigns trying to fill all the same necessaries, and they just end up collapsing right back into overseers with another label. Then what, we're doing it 'cuz we don't like the name? We've long pulled the worst teeth from their innards, none of the rigid policing or surveillance, it's not like they're really Dissolution Era anymore. They work fine and the miners are fine with 'em, else they wouldn't agree to it, would they?

We oughta just change what we call 'em. That'd solve everyone's problem.

—widely re-split post on a multi-system cluster network, authorship unknown

---

It took Ro more than his entire off-shift—during which he'd fully convinced himself he was going to die, curled somewhere lost in a corner of vestigial ship—before he managed to find his way back. Dizzy with exhaustion and embarrassment, he plunged out into the welcome suffocation of the ore center.

Late. Late for his shift.

Late for *work.*

An Overseer's mouth pitched up right in his path. Ro gave a flail that was the equivalent of an oral squeal and lost his orientation.

Explain, it flashed.

I TRANSGRESSED, Ro said hurriedly. I TRANSGRESSED! I DISAPPOINT.

Explain.

LOST, Ro said. I WAS LOST, THEN I WENT BLUEWARD WHEN I SHOULD HAVE GONE ROUNDWARD AND I WAS ALL THE WAY TOWARD SPACE AND THEN—

If you are ill, correction will be arranged.

Correction. The word tried to snag on Ro's anxiety and dread, on the ominous answers from You-Outside—forever and a shift change ago—but he couldn't pay attention, because words were suddenly rearranging in his head and connecting, with stunning incandescence, like a double-sun day on Orro—

I FIGURED IT OUT! The understanding crashed through every nerve, electrifying him. I FIGURED IT OUT, REDWARD, BLUEWARD, ROUNDWARD, DENSEWARD!

Not my purview, flashed the Overseer. *If you are ill—*

Ro wasn't listening. He couldn't wait to put this in a report! *The seemingly random directional etymologies correlate with the Star Eater senses*, flared the draft in his mind. *For example, it is known that their visual organs can differentiate color wavelengths in excess of 12,000 times the number seen by Ponto eyes . . .*

Searing white light flooded his Star Eater vision. The Overseer.

Worker! Attend to your duties or illness will be declared.

Ro could not have said how a flashing autonomous language had tone, but the Overseer was shouting, shouting at him, with a word for "illness" that was suspiciously close to the Overseers' phrase for "flaw." Fear finally connected in Ro's brain.

Illness. Correction.

But the Overseers weren't supposed to threaten, weren't supposed to embody anything but guidance and expectations, not anymore—so everyone said—

Ro tried to scurry past, raking his senses for You-In-Front until he found her moving as a drag net with one of the larger worker groups. He cast about, looking for where to go, anywhere, with the only answer the same wrathful Overseer.

WHERE DO I JOIN? Ro strove for contriteness, attaching as many humble affixes as he could jam in. I DISAPPOINT, PLEASE DIRECT ME . . .

The Overseer's dark maw loomed. Then it called to a passing spotter. *You. Take on this worker. Proceed.*

It moved away, paying him no more mind—and the spotter's appendages kicked back from Ro in disgust.

The same Star Eater he had crashed into during his first work shift. Of course.

In that moment, Ro ludicrously wanted nothing more than for his body to be able to cry.

You-Behind's team was just heading for extraction. Ro was left drifting in space with her, momentarily alone. Her appendages splayed out sharper than the others, in inky spikes—whether in natural anatomy or intentional posture.

STAY OUT OF OUR WAY, she ordered him.

I UNDERSTAND. You-Behind tended to run large, efficient teams. If he interfered with her work again . . .

WHAT WERE YOU SPEAKING OF? she demanded abruptly.

I—WHAT YOU SAID, Ro stammered. I WILL STAY OUT OF THE WAY—

TO THE OVERSEER. YOU SPOKE OF FIGURING OUT. FIGURING WHAT?

Ro hadn't yet internalized how public a gestural language could be. No such thing as hearing distance, and Star Eaters never had their backs turned.

NOTHING. IT WAS NOTHING. He tried frantically to remember how acceptable it would be not to answer. I FIGURED OUT WHICH WAY I SHOULD HAVE GONE, WHEN I GOT LOST. THAT'S ALL.

You-Behind pulsed. Then she signed: *LIAR.*

Ro was too shocked to register it. Too shocked to deny.

LIAR! You-Behind repeated. WHAT DO YOU REMEMBER!

I DON'T KNOW WHAT YOU'RE TALKING ABOUT! Ro sputtered, aided by the sudden truth of it.

YOU LIE. You-Behind swelled, appendages unfurling. YOU REMEMBER, WHAT DO YOU REMEMBER!

One of her tentacles flung out—and Ro felt more than saw something smack across him, burning and wet. He spun, trying to shield himself, his coordination gone. A handful of glittering liquid marbles broke off into the lack of gravity, gleaming as they quivered.

It took several rapid levels of deduction to comprehend that You-Behind had, essentially, spit on him.

I DON'T KNOW, I DON'T KNOW! Ro's words slapped against each other in their haste. I'M IN CONFUSION, WHAT DO YOU WANT?

Cease immediately! The Overseers, descending—Ro would have thought he should be relieved at their presence, but angry colors flashed from their wide muzzles until it was all he could see. *Return to work!*

Ro contorted in space, trying to comply, but where should he go? Surely they would move him from You-Behind's group? Or send her away, or—

Your confusion remains disruptive. Remove yourself from this shift, an Overseer ordered Ro.

IT WASN'T MY CONFUSION, he tried. I DIDN'T—

Its maw filled his vision.

Remove yourself from this shift. Or illness will be declared.

Ro's mind blanked as if every thought had been snuffed out. He curdled in on himself and obeyed.

You-Behind had moved away, toward her workers. Ro could feel her glaring after him, even as she sailed in the opposite direction from where he slunk numbly out of the ore center.

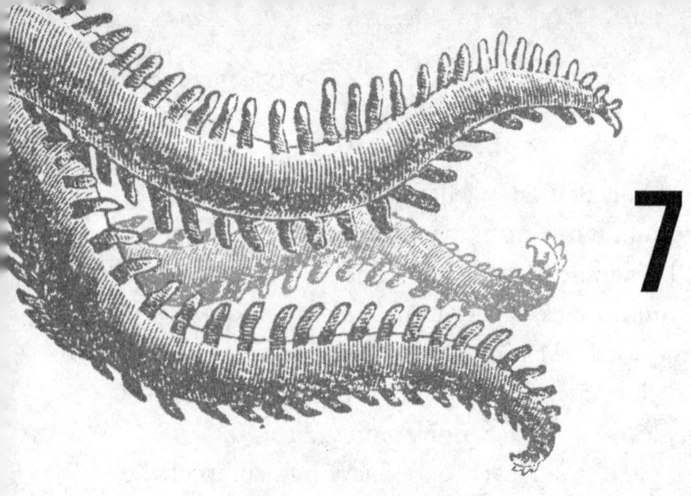

7

A Word That Means Friend, but What Does Friend Mean

The seemingly random directional etymologies correlate with the Star Eater senses. For example, it is known that their visual organs can differentiate color wavelengths in excess of 12,000 times the number seen by Ponto eyes. Unlike in Ponto senses, those colors do not blend into intermediate shades, but are all perceptible as small individual tiles.

In the native Star Eater nebular environment, color would have provided easy directional referents. This Linguist recommends investigating the roots of the other physical properties detectable by the Star Eater field senses—words such as "denseward" are likely an expression of the Star Eater gravitational field sense.

These meanings have been diluted over time, doubtless thanks to the shift to shipboard environments. But someone should write a paper on this!

—Ro, Orro Linguist, Report #004 post-Jump

Ro went back to the cells. You-Outside floated by their usual bays.

She didn't seem to notice or care why Ro would return in the middle of his shift time. No nosy questions, no concern. The usual Star Eater detachment.

MY CONFUSION, Ro felt the need to explain anyway. I AM SENT TO REST.

She twitched slightly in response.

After that, Ro had no choice but to retreat into a cell.

But rest eluded him. After steeping in distress and self-recriminations until he could no longer stand it, he roused himself to the work of making some nexus beads. Including, to his shame, several libraries that ought to be able to bring up filter overlays for the collector, ones that would show guidance paths and directions.

One lost panic too late.

He comforted himself by figuring out how to drop his first reports, anonymous bubbles in the nexus stream that only Orro would know to seek out. Even with You-Outside's directions, navigating the nexus was mentally exhausting, a barrage of overstimulation that Ro was glad to detach himself from once he'd spent his observations.

Orro would hear from him upon the next sync. At least he'd done *something* he was supposed to.

When someone poked around the edges of his cell, he thought at first it must be You-Outside. But she had vanished, and You-In-Front was waving her fronds at him.

The shift had changed.

ALL RIGHT? You-In-Front asked.

UNBOTHERED, Ro said, although he had rarely been more bothered. I TRANSGRESSED.

ONLY ONCE, she said with apparent cheer. VERY BADLY THOUGH. NEXT TIME DON'T BE LATE.

I WON'T. Ro tried to ignore how often in his life he'd been late without meaning to. WHAT OF THE ONE WHO ATTACKED ME? WHAT DEEP OFFENSE DID I COMMIT?

THAT ONE CAN BE STRANGE, You-In-Front said.

She inflected the Star Eater's pronoun with a pejorative. Something like *that-one-who-is-made-of-sour-taste.*

Ro had never heard it in real life. His mood buoyed, shivering in cheeky appreciation.

THAT ONE HATES ME, he said, though less bitterly than he might have a moment ago.

HATE? NO, JUST STRANGE, You-In-Front corrected him. Ro had momentarily forgotten the word *hate* didn't apply to animate beings—Star Eaters didn't hate. Except You-Behind really, *really* did.

At least she was the one people found odd for it, and not Ro.

I HEARD WHY YOU MISSED SHIFT, You-In-Front continued. SOME OF US WISH TO WANDER. I DO, TOO.

I DIDN'T MEAN TO, Ro tried to explain.

OF COURSE NOT. WORK IS LIFE.

WORK IS WORK, Ro said, back on solid ground. So to speak.

WOULD YOU LIKE TO SEE MY FAVORITE PLACE? You-In-Front asked. DON'T WORRY. I WON'T LOSE YOU.

The end of the sentence wriggled playfully, like she wanted him to react. She'd used the intransitive form of the verb—the same one he'd used to say he got lost himself—but embedded against him as a direct object. Not even Ro's fellow Linguists had appreciated wordplay that way.

Next to You-In-Front's natural springiness, all of Ro's mistakes somehow felt less dire.

THE OVERSEERS WON'T MIND? he said cautiously. I DON'T WISH TO DISAPPOINT AGAIN.

OUTSIDE OF SHIFT! THEY HAVE NO CONCERN. COME.

"Not our purview," he supposed the Overseers would say. As long as the workers showed up on time, and functioned, and mined.

Ro followed You-In-Front from the cells. They moved away from the ore center, back toward the dark recesses of the enormous grid. Its bars faded before and behind them, sparking a residual nervousness in Ro. But he had the maps this time, and You-In-Front zipping confidently beside him . . .

And now that he was no longer shackled by panic, he was continuously surprised at how clearly he could perceive their surroundings. The Star Eaters could see in much lower light—plus his electromagnetic senses, and vibrational senses, and so much more that filtered in to combine and enhance his mental picture. It was starting to happen without conscious thought.

You-In-Front led him far from the populated areas, until they began to pass pitted pillars and crossbars. Or hanging panels, or broken elbows, or once-solid bulkheads of more closed rooms that had now become as open as the rest of the grid.

MOST OF THE SHIP IS AGE-OLD, You-In-Front said. WE USE ONE PART OF HUNDREDS.

That aligned with what Ro had been taught. The Star Eaters had once been much greater in number.

And maintaining a prison would have taken significantly more power. Force fields, and more Overseers, and surveillance, and . . .

THE LABORATORIES, You-In-Front said.

They hovered for a moment, staring down a gallery of alcoves, some with more walled configurations and others open. Ro could not have guessed at a purpose for most of the ghostly equipment that stabbed out of corners.

MEDICAL? he hazarded.

SOME OF THEM, You-In-Front answered, unreadable.

They moved on. Past defunct power centers, and darkened banks of equipment, and racks of capsules that had once been capable of maintaining atmosphere. That wouldn't have been for the Star Eaters' benefit.

WHAT DOES HAPPEN, IF WE ARE ILL? OR INJURED? Ro asked, thinking of the labs. *Correction will be arranged*, the Overseer had said. *Illness will be declared* . . .

MANY SCIENTISTS STILL REQUEST STUDY OF US, You-In-Front answered. IF NEEDED, THEY WILL SEND FOR ONE SUCH, BY ASTRAL POCKET.

The Star Eaters were bodily robust, with minor regenerative capabilities. But in injury, they would be overseen by a foreign scientist.

Or in "illness." Presumably on the word of the Overseers.

WE HAVE NONE OF OUR OWN MEDICS? Ro asked.

You-In-Front only quirked toward him, the equivalent of an odd look. WORK IS LIFE.

WORK IS LIFE, Ro said, hiding his dismay.

He lost track of how long they swam through the ancient lattice. You-In-Front led him through the maze to where the light began to take on an imperceptibly different quality. Ro could not have put a name to what he was sensing until, with shockingly little warning, the grid seemed to unfold away, opening and spilling out into—

Space.

Empty space. And distance. And stars. They'd reached the outside of the collector.

For a brief beat of time Ro could have sworn he was about to fall, fall and fall and fall forever, even though they'd stopped moving. He reflexively wrapped a quarter of himself around the final bar of the grid.

MY FAVORITE SPOT, You-In-Front said.

Ro could see why. One couldn't drift here without the aching infinity of the universe permeating every membrane.

They soaked it in together, quietly.

Then You-In-Front asked, HAVE YOU TRIED SEEKING MERIDIAN AT DISTANCE?

NOT YET, Ro said.

I WILL SHOW. AS BEFORE. WE MUST BEGIN TOGETHER.

To trigger those inborn intuitions—their minds together, in sync with the meridian dimension. Ro perked up, the idea of it sparking through him. Without the pressure of the ore center, he was relaxed, even eager.

Ready. To see what no Ponto ever could.

FIND THE ELEMENT AROUND US, You-In-Front murmured. Her presence pulsed over the vacuum between them. FIND ITS EDGES, HOW IT PRESSES ON SPACE. THEN FIND THE DISTANCE BEYOND THAT. AND BEYOND.

Tiny puffs of meridian glimmered around them. Ro let himself drift into it, tingling with the element's beat against time and space and gravity.

FOLLOW NOW, You-In-Front said. YOU WILL BEGIN KNOWING ITS SHAPE. USEFUL, IF YOU LOSE YOURSELF IN THE SHIP AGAIN, YOU CAN REACH FOR ITS LANDSCAPE! ALWAYS HERE. ALWAYS FAMILIAR. NOW FOLLOW OUT . . . OUT . . .

No matter how many times Ro had listened to the explanations, he had never wrapped his mind around how Star Eaters could sense meridian from thousands of light-years away. "It's not that rare a thing for a species to have some kind of instant sense," Lalo had tried to explain. "Like the electromagnetic fish on Wootten. They put out a field, and *bamp*! They know what's around them, no time between. Or us, too! The Ponto empathic sense is completely instant, it just has to be in range."

The concept of linguistic jumping probably would have blown up Lalo's assumptions about Ponto empathic range.

But the reasoning, as Ro understood it, was the same: that in none of those cases were they sensing the information directly, so much as interpreting the physical fields that enveloped every living and nonliving thing. That logic didn't strike Ro as filling in all the holes, but he was no physicist—and the scholars swore it made sense, if one could understand. He'd asked Lalo in as many ways as he could manufacture, and she'd always answered with a lot of elaborate words like "manifold embedding" and "isotemporal hypersurface."

Ro had a suspicion that the physicists didn't fully get it, either.

WITH ME, said You-In-Front. FOLLOW . . .

For once, Ro didn't chastise himself for his mental wandering. He could keep trying, here, for as long as he needed, in the embrace of space and senses until further webs sprang up in the background—and more—and more—

Not something he *saw,* but another sense entirely, an extrapolation of his brain that grew real and tangible and *startling*—

Ro's appendages whipped in glee and shock.

FARTHER! You-In-Front spurred him. KEEP ON!

It was like he stood on a soaring pinnacle and could gaze anywhere in the galaxy.

Not a galaxy he recognized, no constructed context overlaid: Ro couldn't have said which way Orro lay, or whether any twining web of meridian fell near a government or civilization. Only the natural landscape unfolding around him into forever, fathoms of the fathomless.

Ro had never felt so small in such a stunning, shining way. As if he could hold the whole massive infinity of the universe within his mind, and—

And it was gone.

I LOST IT, he gasped, grasping after the memory. But the black stayed empty, the pinpricks of stars untouchably distant.

NO ONE CAN KEEP IT LONG, You-In-Front said. MOVING TO A NEW HARVEST GROUND TAKES MANY MINDS.

Ro and the others would guide the ship out when the time came. He'd known it, but now it towered in his future with apprehension and awe. Far Pre-Dissolution, Star Eaters had always been bodily necessary for a meridian jump. But technology and star maps had allowed other beings to work the element for their needs, melding it with celestial navigation once it was in this dimension . . . except for when it was more meridian itself they sought.

Then, all the workers on the collector would make its jump the ancient way. Their consciousnesses gently hooking into the same spot, a distant target only their senses could find in the deep. They'd leap together as the Star Eaters of old, bringing the collector with them.

Star Eater field senses had no easy translation to galactic coordinates.

JUMPING IS WHEN THE ELEMENT CAN BE VOLATILE, You-In-Front said. SINCE WE USE SO MUCH, TO BRING THE SHIP. BUT DO NOT FEAR. YOU WILL HAVE MANY MINDS TO FOLLOW AFTER. THE OTHERS WILL GUIDE.

I DON'T FEAR, Ro said, and found it was true. Accidents had hardly ever happened. But more than that, his perception of the meridian's instability and danger was calming next to this new idea of it—as a magnificent part of the natural world, a neutral phenomenon that would keep its benevolence as long as they respected it.

They could bring the ship anywhere.

They could bring *themselves* anywhere. If they chose to.

DO YOU EVER WISH FOR SOMETHING DIFFERENT? Ro said.

He wasn't supposed to ask anything like that. But how could a being not wonder? And You-In-Front was so unexpected, so cheery and curious and approachable . . .

DIFFERENT HOW? she said.

IN LIFE. A DIFFERENT LIFE.

She paused a moment. THIRD SHIFT? SOMETIMES I WISH TO CHANGE TO THIRD SHIFT.

WHY THIRD SHIFT? Ro asked.

IT'S THIRD, You-In-Front said, with the frilling that Ro had gathered meant she was trying to be funny.

The worst part of not having a full grasp of the language was that Ro couldn't tell when he didn't get a joke versus when it was just a bad one.

He should have known that would be the answer, though. No Star Eater had ever strayed.

DO YOU WISH A DIFFERENCE? You-In-Front said.

Ro ought to have left it. But here in the stars and the vastness and the cradle of You-In-Front's full spirits, he felt just daring enough. I WISH TO BEAR YOUNG. SOMEDAY.

THAT'S NO DIFFERENT, she scoffed. YOUR BODY WILL KNOW WHEN.

That unvarying, uncrackable nut of the Star Eater response, here in front of Ro in real life!

WHAT IF IT DOESN'T? he pressed. FOR ME?

THEN IT DOESN'T, she said. She was starting to seem puzzled—he had pushed too far. COME, LET'S RETURN. YOU DON'T WISH TO BE LATE AGAIN.

WORK IS LIFE. Ro had never said it more fervently. He never, *ever* wanted to be late again. THAT OVERSEER WAS WATCHING ME FROM BEFORE, TOO. I MUST NOT DISAPPOINT.

You-In-Front paused in the midst of moving back into the collector, her core in shadow.

WHAT OVERSEER?

IT ASKED ABOUT ME, DIDN'T IT? Ro said. BEFORE OUR FIRST SHIFT TOGETHER. IT'S STILL BEEN WATCHING.

IT'S STILL WATCHING? In all their conversations, You-In-Front had never felt this riveted on him. It was unsettling.

ALL SHIFT, Ro said. UNTIL THIS ONE, BECAUSE I WAS LATE. . . . YOU DIDN'T SEE?

I DID NOT LOOK PAST THE MINING. Various ends of You-In-Front tensed inward. I DIDN'T SEE.

I MUST IMPROVE, MUSTN'T I? Ro said. WHAT HAPPENS IF I DISAPPOINT AGAIN?

YOU WON'T, she answered.

BUT IF I DO?

DON'T.

It was all she would say. For the rest of the way back, she seemed distracted, barely responding to any of Ro's attempts at engagement.

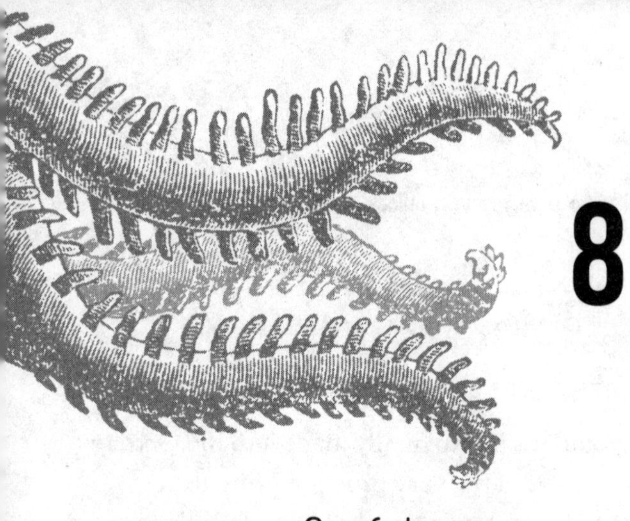

8

Confidence.
Arrogance.
Hubris.

The first scholar to study Star Eater reproduction was conglomerate field scientist Sayl d'Chifte Hausht. Medical research done during Dissolution has come under question in modern times, but judged within the permissibility of its era, Sayl's research respected standard ethical guidelines and partook in none of the crueler experimentation on regeneration or limb severing that were exposed later.

Regardless of modern moral argument, Sayl's influence on our knowledge of Star Eater biology cannot be overstated. Nearly all standard translations of Star Eater physiological or anatomical terms can be traced to Sayl's Dissolution Age research, and all study since has built on those initial breakthroughs. Sayl's descriptions of the Star Eater budding cycle remain among the most detailed records of the process, and loom ever larger in the field considering the depleted opportunity to make new observations.

Opinions on Dissolution medical experimentation notwithstanding, we owe a great debt to such a thorough and brilliant mind. Many

wish Sayl were alive today to unlock a solution to the Star Eater reproductive crisis.

—Portrait of Dissolution: A Capsule Collection of the Era's Major Figures

---

Eight shift rotations in, Ro finally made it to the Orro rendezvous point—tired but very proud of himself.

Sure, it had taken him a few shifts. But he'd figured out the nexus, he'd found his bearings mining, and he'd begun building connections with two separate Star Eaters. (Maybe one and a half. But his reports said two.) He'd rediscovered his anticipation and vigor while learning how to take his early mistakes in stride—which felt like an accomplishment itself!—and he'd managed to roll along without constant anxiety over that watching Overseer. Meanwhile, he'd recorded almost twenty reports so far, with as much detail as he could cram in . . . then spent most of his off-shifts poring over nexus guides of the ship until he figured out how they matched his memorized paths. (Yet another translated interpretation, to transfer the Star Eater augmented map overlays to Ponto landmarked directions. But Ro had put his metaphorical nose to it until he'd figured it out.)

Not to mention that *he had jumped*! His Seniors were going to be thrilled.

Despite the lack of official surveillance, Ro kept his spherical senses on pinprick alert as he picked his way toward the rendezvous point. He gave into his compulsions to double back, or to twist about as he moved, as if one side of him would catch the slither of an Overseer better than another—but no automaton twined through this strand of dingy emptiness.

The astral orb was waiting for him, hanging lambent in a crossing of the grid. Doubtless stationed in place since the moment Ro had sent word of which collector he'd landed in. He would be able to speak to his Seniors, together in real time—he could ask questions, receive guidance and succor, hear news of his family . . .

The white shine of the astral field rippled and expanded at his approach. Ro steadied himself and let his body be swallowed in its pocket. Brightness flashed before a generic starfield appeared, much blanker than the one where he'd joined You-Outside.

WHAT COLOR THE UNIVERSE? asked the Star Eater floating in its center.

Even after such a short time on the collector, the form of the simulation looked fake. Overly smooth. Like the average of a universe worth of expectations.

MOSS TEA AND GRAPPLES, Ro returned the memorized passphrase.

The starfield dissolved into an equally generic Orro cave. A Ponto squatted in its center, an older one, with loose folds of skin and graying fur. Only Ro's Star Eater form remained the same.

The Ponto's mouth opened. "Linguist Ro?"

It was eerie—the sound of the avatar's voice wouldn't have traveled in vacuum, but within the bound particles of the astral pocket, its vibrations rang against Ro's sensitive membranes. A moment of twisty thought to interpret it into words, but the transition was surprisingly fluid.

YES! Ro signed. YOU FOUND ME!

"You're late. You are addressing Master Linguist Koa."

Ro's innards contracted. A Master Linguist? They existed in a barely conceived reverence, far above even the Warren instructors. Ro instinctively tried to straighten in the direction of the illusory gravity.

MASTER LINGUIST. I SEE YOU.

"Seen." The Master Linguist's nose wrinkled. "The accepted Star Eater translation is the weak declarative of the transitive form of *to witness*."

Had Ro known that? He made a quick gesture acknowledging the mistake and guessed at the right word in Star Eater. I WITNESS YOU, MASTER LINGUIST.

Master Linguist Koa sniffed. "We have received your reports."

I HAVE SO MUCH TO ADD, Ro said. THE DEICTIC AND SEQUENTIAL TIME REFERENCES ARE SO IDIOSYNCRATIC, IT'S NOT THE WAY OTHER SYMMETRIC SPECIES CONCEIVE TIMELINES RADIALLY OR IN SPIRALS, OR LIKE US, EITHER, WHO GO IN THE DIRECTION OF OUR WRITING! THEY CHART RELATIONAL TIME IN ALL OPPOSITE DIRECTIONS OR DIAGONALLY—OR SOMETIMES THEY REVERSE IT IN THE SAME CONVERSATION—AND THE REBRACKETING, I THINK A LOT MORE REBRACKETING MAY BE HAPPENING WITH THE BORROWED WORDS THAN WE'VE ACCOUNTED FOR BECAUSE—

"*Silence!*" Koa roared. "You disgrace the Warren. This should never have been you!"

Ro's body went flaccid.

He'd jumped.

He'd *jumped.*

The premiere accomplishment of any Linguist. His

first contact with Orro ought to be pride and relief and happiness—

"This is what desperation breeds." The Master Linguist might have been spitting at a sewage pit, so plain was his distaste. "No one with your record ever should have been allowed to continue training. 'It couldn't hurt,' they argued, not with your *potential*, we needed a jump too badly. And what were the chances it would be any one Ponto, let alone *you*! A beneficial problem to happen, it was claimed—in hindsight, a disaster."

I'M NOT— I'VE BEEN TRYING. Ro's words had gone small and muted. His insides began to sting, as if flea ants crawled through him.

"Ah, yes, shall we review?" Koa's lips curled back. "Per your own reports, you have barely arrived and have already crashed a mining operation, missed work due to your own ineptitude, made at least six major cultural errors that you allowed others to notice, provoked suspicion in an Overseer, provoked another Star Eater into an altercation, and engaged in several interactions that you were warned *over and over* are culturally transgressive."

I DISAPPOINT, Ro jerked reflexively.

"Your apologies change nothing."

I HAVE BEEN LEARNING, Ro said. He inflected it with the humble affixes, trying not to sound defensive. I CAN IMPROVE, I WILL DISCOVER MORE, WITHOUT TRANSGRESSING. MY REPORTS—

"Your reports are not worth tunnel dirt. You fancy yourself an analyst, but that is not your job, Linguist Ro. You do not *think*. You *report*."

Ro's membranes shivered as if a claw had driven in.

YES, MASTER LINGUIST, he managed. OUR UNDERSTANDINGS OF THE CULTURE ARE IMPORTANT. I WILL DO BETTER.

"We understand their culture perfectly. It's you who are failing to follow that understanding."

We don't though? Ro thought. *We can mimic them, but we don't understand at all . . .*

"You are to stop engaging with the workers," continued Koa. "Once you have proven your ability to maintain cover, we will instruct you in methods to conceal meridian on your person while mining. Your only worth in this position is your ability to equalize distribution to Orro."

I'M HERE TO STEAL? The motion bled his dismay. He couldn't help it.

"You are here to help keep *your people* alive. It is to your luck that you still have an opportunity to mitigate this disgrace."

Ro vaguely remembered his Seniors talking about "equalizing meridian distribution." He'd always assumed they meant through information—ferreting out other people's corruption, correcting injustices, making sure his home was granted its proper share.

He'd daydreamed through his training an awful lot.

His world spun, his self-perception swinging. He'd known he didn't keep up with the others at the Warren sometimes, but he'd largely thought of his other qualities as making up for it, more or less—he'd get no plaudits for personal organization or hygiene, but how many of his colleagues had his semantic instincts? Even Senior Aga's last chastisement had supported that self-image. *He may not keep the schedule, but look at this work on multiple negation patterns!*, was the sort of evaluation he'd vaguely imagined from his Seniors . . .

In reality, he'd been on the edge of washing out.

You're here now, he told himself firmly. *None of this changes that you have a job to do. Not just for yourself, but for Orro and for the Star Eaters too, and for anyone who could learn from this. You have to work with the Seniors, but they're also stuck with you.*

Any disappointments with each other would have to be got around. For Orro.

For everyone.

Ro flexed himself, pressing his movements to calm. He could show how reasoned, professional, and humble he could be. While still raising a point.

I UNDERSTAND, MASTER LINGUIST. BUT, IF YOU CONSIDER MY REPORTS, I THINK YOU AND THE WARREN WILL ALSO AGREE ON THE SIGNIFICANCE OF—

"Enough! This is not a *puzzle*, Linguist Ro, it is not your pet research project, and I refuse for Orro's survival to hinge on an unseasoned youngling's pedantry obsession!"

IT COULD HINGE ON THAT THOUGH? As Ro said it, he knew it was true. WE MUST UNDERSTAND THE STAR EATERS BETTER! THE POWER OF MERIDIAN IS THEIRS, NOT THE CONGLOMERATE'S. WHAT IF THINGS CHANGE? THEY COULD DEMAND ANYTHING—

"Demands are not in their nature!"

You don't want us studying their nature! Ro squeezed the response back. *Calm. Professional . . . !*

THEY FOUGHT BACK IN THE PAST, he tried instead. WE KNOW SO LITTLE OF THEIR TRUE DESIRES—

"They tasted dominance and decided they didn't have the appetite. This is what you refuse to accept: *The Star*

Eaters are immaterial. You are immaterial. Orro and the meridian element are all you are to concern yourself with. Repeat it!"

Ro had begun vibrating, a burning bite jerking out to the tips of him. At first he thought it was shame, the hot embarrassment of being chastised by a Master Linguist, all of the successes he'd intended to showcase turning to nothing more than ash.

HOW DARE YOU. The phrase was a single sign in Star Eater, an appalled shock, and Ro had made it before he meant to.

The acridity buzzing through him wasn't guilt. Not anymore.

DISMISS ME ALL YOU LIKE, BUT IF THIS IS WHAT YOU THINK OF THE STAR EATERS, IT'S NO WONDER YOU NEVER JUMPED.

The Master Linguist's fur stiffened all the way to spikes.

What would they do if Ro just stopped reporting? He would never do that, of course. His linguistic revelations might not interest Master Linguist Koa, but posterity would build on them; what he did here *was* important—and Orro—

Ro wouldn't deny that the idea of Orro withering, his hive starving, sent a nightmarish stab through him.

Maybe that's what the Warren was counting on.

They have all the power, he'd said of the Star Eaters. *They could demand anything.*

He was the first Linguist to jump in generations.

He had that same power.

The revelation was like stepping off a cliff, dizziness and rushing fear and instant regret—but by then he was gone.

I HAVE A DEMAND, he said.

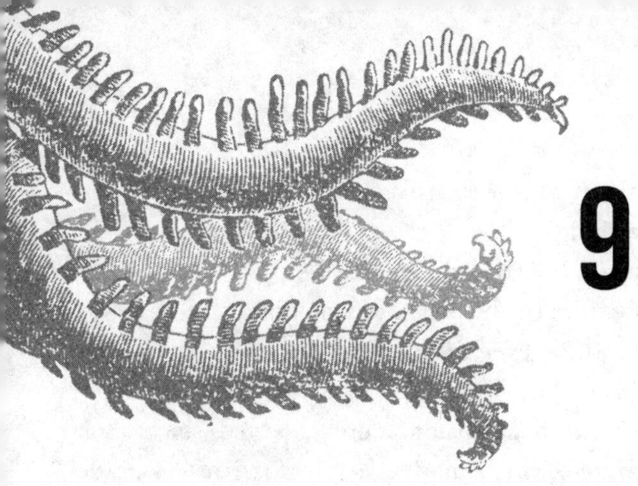

9

The Phantom of Choice, the Illusion of Necessity

Interviewer: Thank you for taking the time to speak with me.

Star Eater: It's no bother.

Interviewer: We're trying to better understand your culture. It's very rare for individuals in any species to be as consistent in their opinions as the Star Eaters are. Even species with genetic caste colony hierarchies or a strongly connected empathic sense always have an individual or two who stray from the norm throughout history.

Star Eater: What is the question?

Interviewer: Why do you think it is, that none of your people ever go their own way? Why does nobody ever decide to leave, or even express disagreement?

Star Eater: Because nobody disagrees.

—*Beyond Meridian: The World of the Star Eaters*, Faragall Interdisciplinary Press Syndicate

---

Ro spent the next few shifts keeping his head down. Just to show he could.

So to speak. If he'd had a head.

They'd *see* him be the bigger person than Koa. A model jumper. He would even follow Koa's orders about interaction; he'd *show* himself the reasonable one . . .

You-In-Front had turned more reserved since their off-shift ramble, which made it easier for Ro to keep to himself. She was still Ro's favorite person to pair with for mining, but now she tended to disappear somewhere as soon as they were released. Ro resisted his natural urge to bridge things and refrained from prodding her.

That wasn't the Star Eater way, as his Seniors no doubt hankered to remind him.

Surprisingly, You-Outside had asked him if he was well, and later she inquired for his help over a few post-confusion questions on procedure or equipment—though she always did it in the abrupt Star Eater fashion, with no lead-in or small talk. Ro was encouraged by the sense that he was making another friend, this time with an impeccable cultural approach. Not one of his interactions with You-Outside could be said to fall outside Orro's strict boundaries.

His reports would be *immaculate.* The Seniors would find not a speck to use against him; he would *show* them.

But in the dark off-shifts, alone with only his own thoughts . . . he swung between wild self-recriminations, the highs of his own empowerment, and straight-up terror.

He'd acted like the ruler of all Orro. What had possessed him?

What can the Warren do to me, though?

But he didn't want to be the kind of person who only evaded consequences because of others' desperation.

Still, an Orro contact who would listen to him . . . that wasn't too much to ask, he consoled himself. Ponto had a word for a person acting entitled above their station, but that wasn't what he was doing, it wasn't. Asking for a different contact—it was, it was *reasonable.*

He channeled the anxiety into recording long observations on morphosyntax and multimodality and exophoric references. He didn't send those as reports, though, not yet.

He had to see who'd be meeting him.

As previously known, Star Eater interrogative, relative, and demonstrative pronouns are unbridled chaos, he rambled into a private record. *Some argue that they don't categorize grammatically as pronouns at all, since many exist as a gestural suffix attached to the abstract concept. "Why" might be "what reason" or "what argument," or "when" might be "what schedule" or "what timing"—but that can be mixed with "what method" or "what steps," in cases Ponto would translate as "how." What the existing research understates is how conflated they appear to be in the Star Eaters' natural use. I wonder at the possibility that this has developed into an intentional linguistic ambiguity, in order to privilege the interpretation of the respondent—but I admit the most likely explanation to be my own flawed knowledge, as the Star Eaters do not seem to enter into frequent misunderstanding. It is proving easy enough to behave as if any answer given is the one my question aimed for, but I am concerned with catching when my own responses may mismatch what is asked . . .*

Or, during his next off-shift: *The unruliness of Star Eater morphosyntax has been commented on at length, but the extent cannot be fully comprehended from outside. I am suspicious I am seeing drift in real time. Take Star Eater adpositions—it is known that some prepositions have shifted in word order to become postpositions and back, but I have observed both usages simultaneously, with the same adpositional affix . . .*

Or, a dashed-off distraction that almost made him late for work a second time: *Used a nexus library to look up the Star Eater word for "quota." Results frustrating to sift through. Etymologically it comes from an expression for "how much" or "how many"—and as mentioned the interrogatives and demonstratives are a fine mess! Anyway, it means exactly what I thought it did. MUST FIGURE THIS OUT.*

After spending far too long following the research tunnel that last one led down, he sailed into the ore center far too fast—and narrowly missed colliding with You-Behind. Again.

Still, he was on time! And Ro decided that plus the fact that he *had* avoided the collision meant this shift belonged in the victory column, which in turn meant he'd almost made it to his next Warren rendezvous without a single cultural incident.

Almost.

You-In-Front caught up with him after shift, once they'd escaped the vicinity of the Overseers. Some of her ends were patting against each other like she was nervous or self-conscious. Ro could have sworn she was more focused on watching back where they had come from than concentrating on him.

HAVE I HELPED YOU? she asked.

Ro was still getting used to how Star Eaters jumped in without the nibbling about or greetings. It went with the lack of discourse markers, he supposed.

YES, he answered. YOU'VE BEEN THE HIGHEST HELP.

I WAS SUPPOSED TO STAY MORE. The wringing of her appendages grew more frantic. WITH YOU. I WAS SUPPOSED TO STAY. I DIDN'T KNOW. I TRANSGRESSED.

Oh, no—had she gotten in trouble for when he got lost? What if they were blaming her for his cultural blunders, everything the Master Linguist had warned him about? What if they assumed he'd gotten it all from her? It had never occurred to Ro that his stumbles could fall on another.

IF THE OVERSEERS ASK, You-In-Front said, WILL YOU SAY I STAYED? WILL YOU SAY I WAS WITH YOU?

WHAT SHIFT? Ro asked.

ANY. IF THEY ASK, WE WERE TOGETHER. I TOLD THEM WE WERE . . .

Discomfort twinged in Ro. Covering for someone with an Overseer felt like willfully wading into an eel pool. But how could he say no?

OF COURSE, he answered, striking the words more firmly to make up for his hesitation.

You-In-Front's nervous motions stilled. YOU DO ME A GREAT SERVICE.

The Star Eater version of thanks—a statement of the received action.

Ro clamped down on a thousand questions. The Master Linguist would have applauded his restraint—until the thousand-and-first slipped out.

IF WE DID NOT OBEY THE OVERSEERS, he said, WHAT WOULD HAPPEN?

Culturally transgressive, *horribly* culturally transgressive . . .

You-In-Front looked blank. WHY WOULD WE NOT OBEY THEM?

Ro might have transgressed further by pointing out that she'd just asked him to lie for her, but he'd become distracted. Caught on parsing the question. The awareness of his recent notes crowded through his brain—because she had said *why*.

Except that it might equally be *How could we not obey them.* Or *In what way would we not obey them.* Or *What do you mean by not obeying them* . . . The literal translation was more like *we-not-obey-them-what-explanation*, and it had registered as *why* without translation in his brain, but *what if that was wrong*?

It was the first time he'd caught the ambiguity of the question in the moment, instead of reconstructing it from an oddness afterward.

He extricated himself from the interaction in a daze and made it to his rendezvous, almost late. When the astral orb's pulsing light appeared and jerked him back to the present, his anxiety reared back up in a rush—he'd been so absorbed by the question about interrogatives that he'd momentarily forgotten he was about to get a different type of answer—

His demand. His brazenness.

He had a moment of near-liquid fear, convinced Master Linguist Koa was about to appear and rain down some unimagined fury.

Then the astral field wavered and swelled, popping Ro into an Orro cave with a puffy, elderly Ponto.

MOTHER HOBI! Ro cried.

He went wet with relief. He'd thrown out her name with

abandon, a reckless ask in the midst of a more reckless one. But he'd barely dared hope they'd assign someone new, let alone the exact name he'd requested. Mother Hobi was qualified and cleared for such a role, but a wide distance from being a Master Linguist.

Clearly Koa hadn't wanted to deal with Ro, either.

Or maybe Ro had more power than he'd thought.

"Ro!" Mother Hobi's face widened in joy, so much that Ro imagined he could still feel her aura doing the same. "You did it, tottie. You did it!"

I DID IT, Ro said, a happy glow blooming in him. This—this was all he had wanted.

"You've got them all in a tizz aboveground," Mother Hobi said.

YOU'RE NOT IN TROUBLE, ARE YOU? Ro hadn't thought to worry about that.

She flicked a claw. "I've navigated Warren politics for decades. I sip their trouble with honey. Now tell me everything."

Mother Hobi was much more accommodating to Ro's scattered dashing from point to point. She did corral him off his linguistic discoveries faster than he wanted ("Time enough for that later"), but she quivered in shared delight at Ro's notes on collocations ("Flexibility of ordering within an idiom is quite unusual!") and was more than willing to give him news of his hive ("They miss you—they were told only that you were chosen for special assignment").

"But we must concentrate first-most on bringing your training up. Ro, the Seniors may have bent to you this once, but there is immense pressure from above. On both of us."

MASTER LINGUIST KOA WANTED ME TO STEAL MERIDIAN, Ro said. THAT CAN'T BE OUR PURPOSE, CAN IT?

Mother Hobi hesitated. "Every body politic in the conglomerate participates in black-market meridian trade. Desisting would stop nothing, only harm those we love."

BUT JUMPING, Ro cried. IT'S SACRED, IT'S MAGNIFICENT, IT SHOULD BE USED FOR SOME HIGHER MEANING! NOT—NOT THIS . . .

"My dear Ro. I wish we could live according to the idealism of your youth. But philosophy is a luxury when measured against Orro's survival. Our Primaries try to shield the hives from how fragile Orro's resource balance is, but the jumps . . . the jumps have been our only advantage against the corruption of much larger powers."

Ro wanted to deny it. But he didn't know how to deny a calculation of fact, other than *It shouldn't be this way.*

Too big for him to push at, or change. Too big for Orro. His entire people was still one of the smallest in the conglomerate.

The history of xenoanthropology was littered with scholars who had researched with ulterior motives, stringing bridges across the universe while also gleaning its resources. The idea that Ro might have striven for enlightenment only to land square in such a bitter, compromised tradition—it left a bad taste in several parts of his body at once.

But he also didn't want Orro to die.

If harm came to Mother Hobi, or Lalo, or his littersisters, or his hive, and Ro had been able to prevent it . . .

"You can continue sharing your cultural observations," Mother Hobi comforted him. "I want to see them, tottie.

You can send them straight to me. You just cannot put them ahead of either staying hidden or your immediate duties to Orro. *Canyah?*"

Pichto Creole. *Are we in agreement?*

It sounded so unobjectionable. Ro should say yes, of course; he was being immature. Pouting. All because he wanted a reality different from this one.

The corners of Mother Hobi's eyes wilted in emotion. "Young Ro. The momentousness of this, the danger—to you, to Orro—I never wished this on you."

I KNOW, Ro said.

"You must keep your awareness about you. Every instant, every thought. This is no practice cocoon, it is a cliff's edge, and your claw cannot slip. Impulsiveness will cost more lives than yours; if the conglomerate discovers what Orro has been about . . ."

Ro wanted to say he knew all that, too, but Mother Hobi was right. Every step could be quicksand, and Ro hadn't been treating it that way.

He could, though. He would.

WHAT ABOUT CONNECTING WITH THE OTHER WORKERS? Ro asked. MASTER LINGUIST KOA SAID I SHOULDN'T . . .

"Koa is correct that you must moderate yourself more. You *must*, for safety, do you hear me? But more cautious relationships can be useful. For instance, the worker you just described doing this favor for—she may be inclined to return the alibi, and the stakes may be much higher for you."

Ro hated to think that way. He didn't want his friendship with You-In-Front to be a trade.

He hadn't wanted to cover for her in the first place. But he didn't want the Overseers to think she'd done something wrong, either, and he didn't want the Star Eaters to be in this messed-up deference to the Overseers or the conglomerate, and he wasn't supposed to think that way because he was projecting a cultural judgment but it just didn't seem *right*—

None of it seemed right.

And Ro couldn't do anything about any of it.

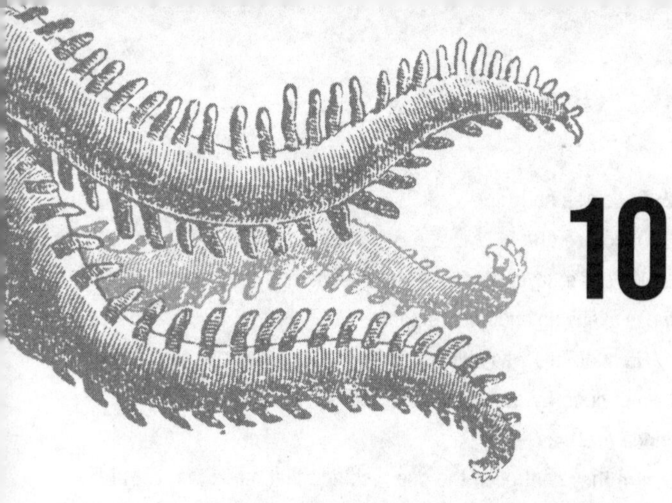

10

If Sacrifice Lacks Meaning, Does It Need a Different Name

Guest: hi top, hi top, thanks! Kkk this is "questions we're embarrassed of" right? Here's something I don't get. How did Dissolution happen? I get that people gakked over the Star Eaters, but why in spacedom would the leaders back then do anything so doof? Didn't they know wiping out the Star Eaters would gak the whole galaxy, too?

Host 1: No no, great ask! So first thing, just as a throw-out, we don't have full-full records from way back then. But the short version is selfishness, and power, and thinking who controlled the Star Eaters controlled it all. Historians mark the beginning of Dissolution Era when Rakyir and Dossania started the invasion, and you can believe they never meant that to go how it did. They wanted to take over the Star Eaters and keep 'em for themselves, not near-up destroy them—

Host 2: But here's another thing that's twitchy to acknowledge, and it's part of why it all went so fray once everyone else shredded in. Pre-Dissolution, when the Star Eaters controlled the meridian element, well, sometimes they were kinda tuckwads about it.

Guest: That doesn't excuse—

Host 2: Of course not!

Host 1: Of course not.

Host 2: No one's saying that nohow. Just setting the curtain. You got these aliens no one understands—

Host 1: No one! This was still in the days when most interpretation was being done by autotranslators, before it came clear what a duck idea *that* was—

Host 2: But they controlled the one resource that made the rest of civilization able to expand an' explode. And yeah, sometimes they were wads. There were times they let refugees get stranded or colonies die out for whatever political reason or other.

Guest: The Star Eaters? Political?

Host 2: Oofya, to extremes. Way different from how they are now, at least from what we got records. They knew they had power and they used it. Gotta some folk angry, gotta other folk desperate, and that's a combo ready to set off like bad orbit fuel.

Host 1: You know though, I'm not convinced our ancestors wouldn't've done it anyway. It's not like the greedy guns who ran Rakyir and Dossania were thinking on any of the domains the Star Eaters gakked over.

Host 2: No, that's a point, they wouldn't.

Host 1: Everyone dove in for their own reasons and then by the end they were war-strung and on their last exhaust, and when they finally went to put down weapons, well, the Star Eaters were still the alien, the other, the resource they'd been fighting over. They made peace with each other by agreeing to control and divide that resource. Greatest moral tragedy in remembered history.

Host 2: And so was born our great conglomerate.

—nexus capture of the farcast *Kicking Straight*

The jeopardy instilled by Mother Hobi helped Ro stay more focused. Get to his work shift, on time. Keep to himself, mostly. Take quiet mental notes that he could express only in reports.

Mother Hobi also forced drilling on the urgent gaps in his training, a regimen Ro meekly submitted to. He spent long off-shifts cramming memorized procedures that he ought to have learned at the Warren. Mother Hobi directed him on the proper decision touchstones to help smooth his linguistic second-guessing, such as skewing toward a vagueness when unsure of an interrogative, so his interlocutor could fit Ro's response to whatever question had been asked.

Ro missed the exhilaration and discovery of more free-flowing conversation, but he had to admit this was safer. Easier.

He told himself he could explore later, cautiously. When he'd figured more out.

His work began to fall into a rhythm. On-shift, off-shift, with the only variation that sometimes the Overseers would announce a visiting scholar or journalist who wished to speak to a Star Eater, the way You-In-Front had mentioned. Ro was under strict orders not to put himself forth for such interviews until he could be certain of passing, but nobody took notice. Someone always volunteered.

(No one seemed particularly enthusiastic about it, though. The visits were treated more like a chore that needed doing, and a worker would offer to spend their off-shift clearing the task. But somebody always did, uncomplaining, in the Star Eater way.)

Ro was all too relieved not to have seen any more Star

Eaters leave for so-called "correction." Mother Hobi and the Warren didn't know much more about it than he did; prior Linguist reports had confirmed only that the missing Star Eaters eventually returned—though sometimes after a lengthy time, and often in the clear midst of a new confusion period. But such absences were, thankfully, rare—of course they were rare; the Star Eater population was too small. Ro managed to worry less and study more.

And when not cramming his neglected training, he spent the rest of his off-shifts exploring the collector—and dwelling on his distaste for the upcoming task.

Stealing meridian. The *dirtiness* of what they asked of him . . . it wouldn't stop chafing, no matter how many rationalizations he repeated. He folded the ugly constraints through his mind over and over, digging for other solutions and hitting claw-sharp realities every time.

Fortunately, he did have one talent playing in his favor: He had great skill at delaying.

Back on Orro, he'd put off tasks for an embarrassing number of cycles just because they didn't interest him. Or had too many steps. Or gave him a twingy need to scurry away and avoid.

Like this one did.

Mother Hobi had begun to prod him, but Ro put her off by claiming he was still working to locate the collector's defunct extractors. He'd need them if he wanted to smuggle out meridian, and he hadn't found one yet that still worked. (He was pretty sure he wasn't starting them right, but he didn't mention that. A lie of omission.)

The next shift started like any other.

An Overseer had flashed an announcement of three

scheduled nexus visitors, an unusually high number—from the Iheyi Sea, Nya-Lachow, and the Khord Confederation. Ro was curious how that worked, since Nya-Lachow was composed of a number of microbial species who formed cumulative intelligences. Maybe their astral pockets let their collectives take on Star Eater avatars to communicate.

Ro stayed obedient, tamped down his curiosity, and didn't volunteer.

You-Behind had been the one to wave in for Khord. It was a bonus to know she wouldn't be lurking anywhere after their work shift and would instead be ticking through some milquetoast interview with one of the conglomerate's largest superpowers. She'd mostly taken to ignoring Ro since their last altercation, which he was more than fine with.

Unbothered, he found himself thinking.

His mind had been reaching for Star Eater automatically more and more of late. Once he couldn't raise the Ponto word for *shift change* until much later.

It was both exhilarating and mildly terrifying.

As usual, he rambled through the grid once he was released from work. With no one around to see, he had taken to touching the lattice joints as he went by, tagging them with one tentacled end and then the next. It wasn't a Star Eater behavior, but he didn't think it was a Ponto one, either. It was more like how, as a Ponto, he'd always had to press his paw pads flat after walking somewhere, which his litter-siblings had found a funny affectation. Or how his mouth had puckered on eating anything mashed, which, culturally, was about half of Ponto recipes, and which was uncannily similar to how his appendages now continually felt too wet for no reason.

Those didn't feel like Ponto things. They felt like Ro things.

He wasn't naive enough to relax about them where anyone could notice. But it relieved some of his crammed-up anxiety to be able to touch the grid. As if he was more in tune with the ship, and himself.

This off-shift began the same way, his appendages moving from one bar or corner to the next in a comforting rhythm. Until he registered the vibrations.

They'd been building for a time. At first a mere buzz of background, thrumming through to where he touched the solidity of the ship, then shaping toward coherence as he got closer. Not the clarity of precise knowledge, not yet, but the tang of impressions—something going on, something unusual—

Something wrong.

Ro couldn't have said what gave him that sense. A staccato, jerking resistance embedded in the tremor? A grating screech reminiscent of claws on ceramic, the sound Oltasol called *frene*? Then spiking against it, the edge of a voice, of oral sound, that made every instinct stand on end even though Ro couldn't hear the words . . . ?

He began to pause, to touch and listen, and then to hurry. He crawled through crevices of the ship he'd never found before: bolted-over corridors, darkened and blocked passages, closing in on wherever those vibrations grew louder and stronger and louder until he burst out—

—into one of the old medical labs.

The blinding bright of an astral field overwhelmed his senses, and then he was inside it. Its contents imprinted on his senses instantaneously.

An overlay on the real-life laboratory. With You-Behind writhing in its center, screaming without sound.

The room's ancient equipment stabbed through her in several directions. She beat against it in clear agony, and floating above . . . a plump, diminutive sugar puff of a being, smaller than a Ponto, with eyes that took up half the face and four tiny hands. A Gormi. One of the dozen most common species in the Khord Confederation.

Ro screamed too, every appendage whipping taut.

He tried to recover and shout *NO* or *STOP* but any words smashed and collided. The Khordian's big-eyed visage snapped toward him and winked out, disappearing instantly along with the nexus overlay.

The lab, and its torture devices, and You-Behind shuddering in their center—they stayed.

Ro rushed to her side.

YOU'RE BACK, YOU'RE BACK. I DREAMED YOU LEFT ME, You-Behind moaned. YOU BECAME SOMEONE ELSE. I WAS ALONE . . .

I'M HERE, Ro whispered. He didn't know what else to say. I'M HERE.

DON'T LEAVE ME AGAIN, she begged.

I WON'T. I WON'T.

He cast about for how to detach the machines. How had the Khordian done this? The astral pockets were only sensory fields, not transport; some far distant outsider couldn't have affected this reality. Couldn't have driven piercing tubes through You-Behind's flesh . . . or the rods that seemed to serve no purpose other than to hold her body down like a mud crustacean pinned to an epicurean board . . .

No instructions to follow, just You-Behind twitching and incoherent and Ro didn't know if he was going to hurt her worse, but he grappled at the mechanical arms and pins and tubes and heaved.

One by one, he managed to draw them out. Globes of black ichor quivered in their place, swelling as more seeped. A few globules broke off, shining grotesquely as they floated.

You-Behind's ceaseless trembling served as a horrific backdrop.

Ro would have given anything for her to stop—until she did. The moment she drifted free, she went still as death.

Ro didn't know what to do.

He had to get her out of here. If they were Ponto, he would have boosted a shoulder under her, but Star Eater bodies were so symmetrical, and so lacking in orientation—and You-Behind so injured—that he blanked on any good equivalent. He wriggled over and reached out. Where they touched, his appendages stuck to You-Behind's with an unpleasant sucking.

As delicately as he could, he nudged and tugged until he was towing them toward the cells and people and some kind of help. Carrying someone in zero gravity was no difficulty at all, but Ro had to shuffle with excruciating slowness to keep from banging her into the grid. He kept his senses wide, half expecting the Overseers to descend and drag You-Behind back to that pit of violation . . .

They'd made it about halfway back when she began kicking weakly against Ro.

He melted in relief. He'd not wanted to acknowledge the lurking fear that she might not stir again.

He let go so she could orient herself. She braced against the grid, pulsing and heaving.

Her wounds had begun to close, with that famed Star Eater regenerative speed. Ro watched with a burst of disgust—was this why someone had thought it was *acceptable*? Because so little record would remain upon her body?

You-Behind seemed to become aware of Ro slowly.

IT'S YOU. She said it with enough of a repulsed twitch that Ro could tell she recognized him this time.

He understood now. He'd figured it out.

BEFORE MY CONFUSION, he said. YOU KNEW THIS ONE. DIDN'T YOU.

I WAS OUT OF MY RIGHT THOUGHTS. She contorted into herself. RAVING ONLY. UNIMPORTANT.

IT IS IMPORTANT! Ro hadn't meant his motions to stab so indignant. *The Star Eaters do not form the same deep connections other species do,* his training materials had claimed. *That is how their society can take the confusion periods in stride.*

Wrong. Wrong, wrong, wrong.

YOU HAVE GRIEF, Ro said. FOR THE ONE WHO HAD THIS BODY. YOU MISS ME.

He inflected the "me" as *me-who-used-to-be.*

NO. You-Behind was adamant. UNBOTHERED.

It must be taboo, so appallingly taboo. That must be why no outsiders understood, because no one would admit—Ro imagined how he would feel if You-In-Front entered confusion, and changed, and forgot him. Even with their friendship so new . . . he'd be devastated.

How long had You-Behind been close to the Star Eater Ro used to be? Decades? Centuries?

Guilt washed up in him. His actions, his being here—he

had stolen her family. If he hadn't jumped, it might have been another lifetime before this Star Eater entered a confusion period for real. Another lifetime together with You-Behind, and maybe others.

No wonder she hated his very presence. She couldn't know how right that reaction was. That it truly was his fault.

IN THE ORE CENTER, Ro said, an infinite sadness filling him. YOU ASKED WHAT I HAD SAID. YOU WERE HOPING TO FIND SOMETHING OF YOUR FRIEND.

A FAMILIARITY ONLY. YOU-BEFORE WOULD SOMETIMES . . . BUT IT'S DONE. I SHOULD NOT HAVE THOUGHT IT.

It was as close to an apology phrase as Ro was likely to get from her.

I CAN'T BE WHAT YOU LOST, Ro said. BUT I CAN HELP. HOW DID THEY DO THIS TO YOU? WHO CAN WE REPORT IT TO?

NO TIME. NEVER. You-Behind seemed to be getting her strength back. Ro must have mistaken the interrogative again, as she'd answered a different one—*when* rather than *who*. THERE IS NOTHING TO TELL. I VOLUNTEERED.

NOT FOR THIS! Ro cried. YOU COULDN'T HAVE KNOWN—

I KNEW, You-Behind said. THEY ASKED. I SAID YES.

SAID YES? TO *WHAT*?

TO THE VISITORS, You-Behind said. WE HAVE TO SAY YES. FOR STUDY.

Study. Ro had never imagined what it meant, to study the Star Eaters. All those scholars, the xenobiologists and medical researchers and scientists. All trying to solve the Star Eater reproduction crisis, or replicate their meridian abilities, or at least figure out how they worked . . .

For the good of the galaxy.

THERE MUST BE ANOTHER WAY! Ro insisted. WHO TOLD YOU WE MUST DO THIS? DO THE OVERSEERS—?

UNBOTHERED. You-Behind cut him off. YOU SHOULD NOT HAVE INTERFERED.

Ro was stunned speechless.

THEY NEED THIS. SO I SAID YES. You-Behind still winced and kinked across some of her words, but her conviction was clear. THEY NEED IT. WE MUST.

Was this the Star Eater way, to cater to any request of the conglomerate, just as they worked for that same conglomerate's good until their own deaths? Would *Ro* give himself away if he refused such a thing?

Even if the Star Eaters said yes, no one in the conglomerate ever should have asked this.

Especially if the Star Eaters always said yes.

Did Orro know? Did they condone it? Ro's first reflex was to run to Mother Hobi, demand she take it to the Primaries. They could take an impassioned stand, rise to the rest of the conglomerate—

Nothing. They would do nothing. "*Orro does not have such power,*" Mother Hobi would explain, again. Or: "*We cannot act on anything that would give you away.*"

Ro was sick of hearing it.

IT'S YOU WHO THE OVERSEERS SHOULD DISCIPLINE. You-Behind's floaty haughtiness was back. MIND YOURSELF AND STOP INTERFERING WITH OTHERS. IT IS *NOT WANTED.*

She flung the last sentence at Ro so hard it was like she had spit at him again. Then she dragged herself away, lurching down the grid in the direction of the cells.

The Star Eaters would never agitate for reform themselves. Not if You-Behind was any representation. *Unbothered*, she would keep saying, *unbothered*, and You-In-Front and You-Outside and all the others would look at Ro in befuddlement and wonder why he, and only he, was bothered.

It's a disservice to the Star Eaters to judge them by Ponto standards, Ro tried to remind himself, but it only succeeded in turning his fury more sour.

He banged his way in the opposite direction You-Behind had gone. He didn't plan to go back to the lab where he'd found her, not in so many words, but he found himself drawn to it. As if it carried its own gravity well.

He gazed across the empty, hollow space. Dark crusts shadowed the spikes and tubes he'd drawn out of You-Behind's body.

I dreamed you left me, she had said. A borrowed word, for a people who didn't sleep. Cribbed from a different gestural language to describe the concept. You-Behind suffered a grief so verboten that she hadn't been able to express it in native Star Eater.

That didn't mean she didn't feel it. That any of them didn't feel it.

A recklessness reared up in Ro. If he could find out what the experimenter had been doing—if he could prove or record the egregiousness of it—he only had to convince the others, of, of something, of the *wrongness*, if they all rose together no one could deny them—he dove across and yanked at the lab's torturous tools, wrenching and bending at them in his fury.

He learned nothing. He didn't have the technical skill

for it, nor the consciousness nor patience to look it up. He wrenched and tore, cracking the unspeakable equipment apart, not even lying to himself anymore about what he was doing, *a lie of comfort, a lie of self.*

Then he felt it.

Buried behind the equipment, under a solid bulkhead—or above it, depending on one's perspective, but smothered away, its whisper barely penetrating out. Ro tore into the panel, prying apart the joints to find what he already knew was hidden. Field-locked balls of it, densely compacted spheres that glittered against each other like perilous jewels.

Meridian.

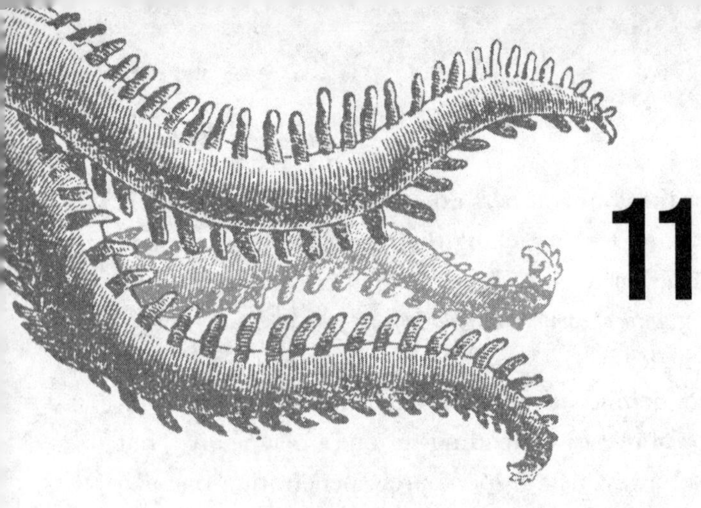

11

Relativity of Space, Relativity of Language, Relativity of Mind

TITLE: *Meridian Gold*

By Kan Kànn. Mixed media.

An artist's depiction of the meridian hypersurface and its immense, imperceptible swoop intersecting our space. Kànn uses minuscule swings of flash-frozen gases to produce a sense of the movement and scale our ships and communications follow when they ride a meridian bubble along the immeasurable hypersurface. Although it can only be tangibly sensed by the Star Eaters, the meridian dimension has inspired countless non–Star Eater artists throughout the ages.

—plaque in the Symphonia Museum of Artistry,
City of Concurrence

Every body politic in the conglomerate participates in black-market meridian trade, Mother Hobi had said.

The Khord Confederation. A behemoth with tens of

millions of worlds, hundreds of thousands of species, and a population of ninety-two quadrillion. They controlled a whole-number percentage of the galaxy's resources and still pushed and pressured for more meridian to come to them, claiming it was deserved, that they exported so many necessities to other, poorer domains and that the galaxy would collapse without their infrastructure . . .

Not incorrect, factually, but that didn't *justify*—didn't give them license to do whatever they wanted, not when they were one of a conglomerate of thousands and only grasped for more and more and more because they were wealthy and huge and they *could*, and had this been their purpose with You-Behind all along?

The incandescence of Ro's rage and helplessness threatened to blank out his senses. He didn't know how densely the attractive forces in field-locks like this would pack the spindles of meridian, but the amount here . . . it wasn't small. They must have been stockpiling it for a long time, and off how many different Star Eaters?

The plan socked into Ro so hard it twanged through his whole body.

Khord had been stealing meridian.

Orro needed meridian.

Khord would never be able to come down on the disappearance of something they shouldn't have had in the first place.

Ro had been so against taking what wasn't theirs, his spirit breaking over least bad options, but if he had to steal . . .

Who better to skim from than the richest domain in the galaxy?

He poked a cautious appendage at the pile, but he'd momentarily forgotten about the lack of gravity. The spheres bobbled against each other and began drifting out of their nest.

Ro grabbed for them and only managed to dislodge several more.

They glided apart from each other like fluffy seeds on an atmospheric air puff. In an instant, ridiculous nightmare, Ro imagined scads of meridian escaping into space, the precious meridian, how many lives—the field spheres were difficult to grab; they had no solidity and squeezed away from him as quickly as he could catch more, not like raw meridian where it would just stick without effort—

That's what I need! The field spheres bobbed all around him now. Ro just needed it to be raw meridian, then he could grab it, he could grab it like he did when mining. But to break that strong of a gravo-magnetic field . . .

Ro scanned hastily, looking for whatever equipment had been used to create and secure the spheres.

He found something better.

A magnetic scoop plate. Of course. They would've needed it to collect the spheres in this trove in the first place. Four of Ro's appendages whipped out at once, turning on the scoop's field and jacking it as high as it would go.

The drifting spheres arrowed in, much too fast, the shortest distance between two points. One grazed Ro, slicing a trough in his outer membrane without slowing.

And every one of the field spheres still in their nested hiding place rose up as one.

Ro had neglected to plan for the undisturbed spheres being attracted as well.

He jerked after them, not sure what he was trying to do. For a moment he thought it would be fine; the spheres had splatted into a tight pile like a spate of amphibian eggs, they were all trapped, no problem . . .

But he'd turned the scoop too high. Or there were too many. Or both.

Ro sensed before he saw as some of the fields began to bleed and blur into each other, like bubbles combining. One sank into the next with the slow inevitability of a coming disaster. He tried to react—but then he felt the first two meridian payloads touch.

They fused in a blaze within Ro's senses, undulating with barely constrained power. No, this was bad, the meridian element was unstable—Ro didn't know how much was in each of the spheres or how much was safe to combine—

The field spheres sucked thin against each other on top, like spreading jelly, and a golden spindle burst through and out, crackling up into the vacuum like it wanted to roar.

Ro dove, trying to catch the meridian on himself like in mining. But more burst out in geysers, some painting Ro in a thick lacquer, others fountaining in arcs, and it wasn't like mining at all, too dense like molten tar that would mire Ro here forever—he spread himself and made a heaving, desperate try to twist the flood up and into him—

And slipped.

Ro's awareness of the meridian schismed, sliding along a parallel infinity of dimensional fissures. Himself, the collector ship, the meridian—veins of it rapidly webbing past him like aquifer ice cracking into a distant underground.

Ro had one more teetering instant when he thought he might be able to block its escape, control it, stem the surge . . .

The moment skidded and plummeted away. Space fractured along the fault lines. Ro's body went inside out. The collector went inside out. Time slowed enough for him to fill with certain horror that they were about to explode into glittering dust across the cosmos.

The collector shuddered and heaved. A screech vibrated through it, soundless and shrieking and loud enough to shred its occupants. The grid careened, crashing into Ro from his redward side.

His senses erupted in supernovas. The collector smashed into his body from another direction. Or he smashed into it.

Reality tumbled around him. Colors flashed, blinding more than Ro's visual sense, and he only belatedly realized they were alarms. He latched on to a corner of the grid and clung. It swung like he was falling, falling forever, and space was endless so the fall would never end . . .

Gradually, everything stilled—though the alarms continued their searing scream, spiking into Ro's consciousness. The space felt different, wrong. Ro couldn't have said how at first, but then You-In-Front's words about the meridian came back to him, how its patterns would orient him.

The collector had moved. They weren't at the mine anymore.

Ro tried to unclench himself from the grid, but his muscles wouldn't react. Parts of him pulsed in a wrong sort of numbness, an absence he didn't want to look at. His imagination flickered, picturing his body half crushed, chunks of him sailing one way while the ship wheeled the other . . .

Achingly, stickily, Ro managed to peel himself free. His limbs were intact. He had a moment of panic that his bracers might not work before they responded. The grid had flipped orientation, and Ro went in circles three times before recognizing which way to go.

The meridian that had burst forth from Khord's stash was gone as if it had never been.

What have I done?

Meridian, the meridian bubbles, they gave access—to another dimension—to skipping through space—and Star Eaters could do it naturally, without any technological help, they only needed, needed meridian—

Jumping is when it can be volatile, You-In-Front had said. *Since we use so much, to bring the ship . . .*

The instability. Ro had been warned.

He'd used the meridian. With no intention, no plan, it had just *happened*, and he'd plummeted with it—wherever it had cascaded—

He'd taken the whole ship with him. Badly.

Parts of the grid had gone warped or hung at angles, ionized arcs sparking before they snuffed out against the vacuum. An increasing number of workers crept and stumbled along the grid as Ro approached the cells, with the odd Overseer clanking abreast of them and barking instructions: *Return to the cells. Return to the cells. An investigation is underway.*

Ro froze in place. An investigation. They didn't know it was him, then, but that might only be temporary.

Belatedly, he wondered if he should run. But where? And how? He'd need more meridian—

A commotion arose down the grid. The knifing blaze of the alarms sent it into planes of shadow and light, wild tentacles and the roiling, serpentine coldness of several Overseers, thrashing in chaos.

Recognition crashed across him. You-In-Front. The Overseers were restraining a struggling You-In-Front.

Ro couldn't move. Couldn't think.

An Overseer dove straight at him, closing the distance with such speed that Ro had no time to react. *You. Was that one with you this off-shift?*

WITH ME? Ro repeated foolishly. He might help by pretending to be You-In-Front's alibi—but if they found out this was his fault, he couldn't drag her down, too— NO, I WAS—

Your answer is understood. The off-shift directly after your confusion, was this one with you then?

AT FIRST, BUT—

He cut himself off, too late, You-In-Front's request echoing in his memory. *Will you say I was with you?*

He'd been too flustered to remember his promise.

Your answer is understood, said the Overseer. *Return to a cell.*

WHAT ARE YOU DOING? MY FRIEND DIDN'T DO ANYTHING! Ro's words weren't coming in the right order. WHAT DO YOU WANT!

Theft and damage are to be punished, it replied. *Return to a cell. Disobey and you will face consequences.*

The Overseer slithered away. Its associates had disappeared into the grid—and with them You-In-Front, snuffed away somewhere he couldn't see.

The Overseers didn't suspect him. Because they suspected her.

Ro slipped into his usual cell. As ordered.

He didn't know what else to do.

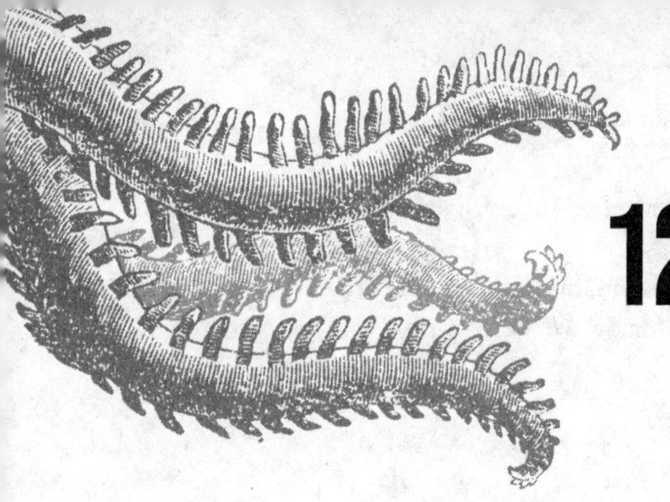

12

Implied, Implicative, Implicated

> dark thought: if the star eaters have genetic memory, does that mean they'll always remember what we did to them?
>
> maybe that's why they stopped having babies
>
> **creepy traumababies. now that's a horror i didn't need with my breakfast**
>
> —public pool conversation excerpted in the introduction to *Mining, Memory, and Outrunning Light: Misconceptions About the Star Eaters*

The Overseers field-locked them inside the cells. Ro should not have been surprised that such a function still worked.

He crept close to the unpleasant buzzing of the field barrier and peered out across the grid. The alarms had calmed, but the Overseers stayed slithering and active, pausing every so often to scan parts of the ship. The astral orbs, too, had been bobbing and swelling, some blurring through into translucent images: bloated eyes or fierce beaks or triple rows of blunted teeth.

Representatives of the conglomerate, stepping in to monitor, intentionally making themselves seen. Demanding an account for what had happened on this collector.

None of Ro's training had covered this. Only that he was never, under any circumstances, to admit to anything that would compromise him—if he made a mistake, *deny, cover, ignore*—

Except the Overseers were targeting someone else, someone innocent, and Orro hadn't anticipated a fallout this bad or it crashing down on someone else . . .

They'd order him to deny it a thousand times harder.

What would the Overseers do to You-In-Front if they thought her responsible? What would the conglomerate do? They wouldn't hurt her, surely. Star Eaters were too valuable . . .

The Khord Confederation hadn't seen it that way.

Ro wrapped his appendages against each other until they knotted and ached. He needed someone to tell him what to do, how to fix this . . . He was as a youngling again, sobbing at a hive mother's knee, begging for an adult to erase his blunders. He recorded an urgent report for Mother Hobi, but it wouldn't send until the next sync, which might not be until after they were set to meet again and that was four full shift rotations away—

Orro would say he couldn't confess. Not under any circumstances. Not even if, if—but when it came to what was morally right—no, he still couldn't give away his whole people! Could he make up some other story, one that explained everything, but gave him a smaller crime? An explanation that didn't implicate anyone, that didn't reveal Orro or the jumps or his true purpose here?

He knew what his Seniors would say. What Mother Hobi would say. Even if he told the Overseers he'd happened upon the meridian accidentally and made a mistake, if that caused them to interrogate him . . . Every tread under the Overseers' brightest focus was a risk that yanked him to the edge. If his own compulsive attempt to set this right snuffed out the lives of every hive on Orro, if the conglomerate's wrath fell upon his home and crushed innocent and guilty alike—

He would never forgive himself then, either.

Wait, wait a little, see what happens, Ro tried to instruct himself. *They can't do anything too bad to her, they can't . . . Seven million people on Orro—!*

Ro cracked a nexus bead to make an astral pocket, wishing for anywhere else, anywhere but here. Then he pulled another, and another. The generic libraries cycled through scene after scene of fake escapes. Expansive astronomical and terrestrial landscapes, boundless cities sprawling across sea or shore or earth or space, abstract artificial worlds of light and gravity and spin . . .

None of it could hide Ro's own reality from him.

His nervous knotting rubbed his membranes against each other until they were raw. Alone, with himself and his thoughts and his guilt . . . it was unbearable.

He pressed up against the wall of the cell and cracked another nexus bead. A quick thought raised the nebular starfield, the one You-Outside had chosen when she'd helped him that first time. He didn't know if the astral field would penetrate the bulkhead, or if she'd be near enough to it, or even if You-Outside had taken her usual cell, but—

She appeared startlingly close, smashed against an invisible wall between them, its opacity filtered out by the augmented reality. Half her body had folded up to cover the other half.

Ro had thought it was he who needed a friend. He'd not had a full idea what *scared* looked like on a Star Eater, but You-Outside was it.

She unfurled slightly, opening toward him.

ALL RIGHT? Ro whispered.

UNBOTHERED, she answered, limbs sagging. STAY WITH ME?

She and Ro each pressed against the borders of their own cell, the slender illusion of empty space separating them.

WHAT WILL THEY DO? Ro couldn't help asking. DO YOU KNOW?

I HEARD THE SHIP WINGED, You-Outside answered. She stopped there.

Ro would have given anything for her to be slightly more garrulous.

At least he had time to parse her response. The interrogatives, tangling him again—he'd dropped most of the grammar in his question, landing on *what-do* and thinking it clear, but she must have interpreted it as *what happened*.

"Winged" wasn't a term he'd heard either. Maybe a borrowed grammatical construction from Haazgi, a contextual reversal of voice and agency: *the room tossed* replacing *the room was tossed.* Or it could have been another calque; in Nahonic or Yotz "wing" could be a transitive error in judgment or a stumbling risk, respectively: *to wing something.*

Or a combination.

The linguistic pressure helped him think, yanking him from the pitted circles his mind had been spiraling into.

WHAT CAUSED IT? he hazarded to You-Outside. DID ANYONE SAY?

WE ARE SOMEWHERE OFF-SPACE. YOU FEEL IT, YES? WE WINGED FAR. By her answer, Ro must have accidentally reversed his question this time, even though he could have sworn he hadn't—*It caused what* instead of *What caused it.* At least he had enough practice now not to be thrown.

YES, he said. WE MOVED . . .

THE BAD BURN MUST HAVE BEEN A GREAT DEAL OF MERIDIAN, You-Outside continued. THAT WOULD MEAN SHIP DAMAGE AND OFF-SPACE.

The waste of a meridian stockpile. The most valued resource in the galaxy. Ro's guilt had temporarily neglected to pile that atop his other calamities.

It would be the gravest sin of all, to anyone who heard. He didn't want to guess how many citizens' survival he'd just shredded, or for how long.

He must not have been able to hide how stricken he felt. You-Outside laid an appendage up against the invisible barrier between them.

WE NEED NOT HAVE FEAR. It would have been more of a consolation if she'd seemed like she believed it herself. IF THE COLLECTOR IS NOT OPERATIONAL, OR WE CANNOT MAKE A STATION, THEY MUST SEND A RESOURCE TOW.

Which meant more meridian squandered, to rescue them. And Ro to blame for all of it.

He pressed several of his own ends across from hers.

I DO FEAR, he whispered. WE CAN FEAR TOGETHER.

Transgressive again. But Ro couldn't solve his own shame and panic, and You-Outside didn't deserve to suffer for it, and helping one other person in this one moment was the only thing he could do.

You-Outside was so still Ro thought she wasn't going to speak again. Then: CAN WE GO SOMEWHERE ELSE?

WHERE? Ro asked.

ANYWHERE. SOMEWHERE LIVELY.

She used a phrase with a connotation of crowds and cheer.

You-Outside was the quietest Star Eater Ro had spoken with, among a species that lived in quiet. But maybe, like him, she needed to not hear her own thoughts.

Ro cracked a new nexus bead, and concentrated.

Their surroundings filled with the aerial urbanization of some unnamed planet, a gossamer city floating across nothing. Nested platforms garlanded through the high dome of a crisply orange atmosphere, their threaded architecture swooping up into the soaring altitude or descending toward an unseen ground. Large, graceful insectoids almost the size of a Star Eater flapped and chattered between structures, their plumage streaming as they flashed inside or out through small pores speckling the infrastructure. The energy of their cacophony poured through the space in a hundred replicated vibrations, their gauzy wings and tails whispering by close enough to feel the breeze of it.

The simulation oddly put Ro somewhat in mind of an Orro hive, though far too high above the ground to be peaceful to him. However, You-Outside relaxed visibly.

Another long stretch of stillness between them. Then You-Outside moved, ever so hesitantly.

WHAT IF THEY THINK WE DID SOMETHING?

THE OVERSEERS? Ro said.

YES. WHAT IF THEY THINK . . . I HAVE BEEN IN CONFUSION. WHAT IF . . .

Emotion crashed through Ro. He wanted to reassure her that an investigation could never wholesale blame the confused, that she'd be fine, because she was innocent—but they might be about to blame You-In-Front for those same crimes, also innocent, which Ro knew because he was guilty, and *why should any of them fear the Overseers anyway*? The Star Eaters were free! It was their own choice how the collectors would be organized! If the Overseers threw punishment upon the undeserved, on You-Outside or You-In-Front or anyone except Ro himself—if they or the conglomerate demanded the Star Eaters' health or bodies or lives—

The Star Eaters *didn't need to submit to them.* Nobody wanted to; why did anyone feel they had to? *They like to work, they feel safe having an authority*, had written hundreds or thousands of research papers on their culture. But You-Outside's nervousness shouted different. You-In-Front asking Ro to lie for her, You-Behind screaming in delirium and agony—they *didn't* like it, they didn't feel safe, and Ro wasn't imagining that—

Why did the Star Eaters need to let *anyone* control them? Or the meridian?

THEN WE LEAVE, Ro said recklessly. IF THE OVERSEERS BLAME THE CONFUSED, THEN WE LEAVE! YOU AND ME AND ANYONE ELSE WHO WANTS TO!

LEAVE? You-Outside looked bewildered. And a little alarmed. WHY WOULD I WISH TO LEAVE?

ANY REASON! Ro cried, deserting every crumb of his carefully memorized training. TO SEE OTHER WORLDS, TO MAKE ART, TO RAISE YOUNG—

WE MAY RAISE YOUNG HERE, You-Outside said. THE BODY KNOWS WHEN.

What the Star Eaters said, what they always said, and Ro was transgressing again, because *he couldn't understand.*

He was here, living among them. And every time he thought he connected, he smashed against the same wall, and he did not understand—if he was caught now he would never have another chance and he had failed at this just as he had at spying and stealing and faking, all the things Orro wanted from him, but also all the higher ambitions he'd asked of himself, because he hadn't made a positive difference anywhere, only destroyed a resource his people depended on to live and plastered his own assumptions over the people he'd committed to learn from. And possibly caused his sins to avalanche down upon an innocent being, a friend, who'd only tried to help him—

Something scratched at the back of his thoughts, but he couldn't pin it down, so lost in the cascade of self-castigations and wretchedness.

ALL RIGHT? You-Outside asked.

UNBOTHERED, Ro managed, stilted. BASELINE . . .

The astral illusion buzzed and flapped around them, packed with vibrance and life. Ro pressed himself tight so it could no longer invade his senses, burying himself against the invisible walls.

Until he glimpsed a rounding of fur and a penetrating eye from behind one bright corner of a simulated platform, piercing into Ro across the thin, sharp sky.

Mother Hobi.

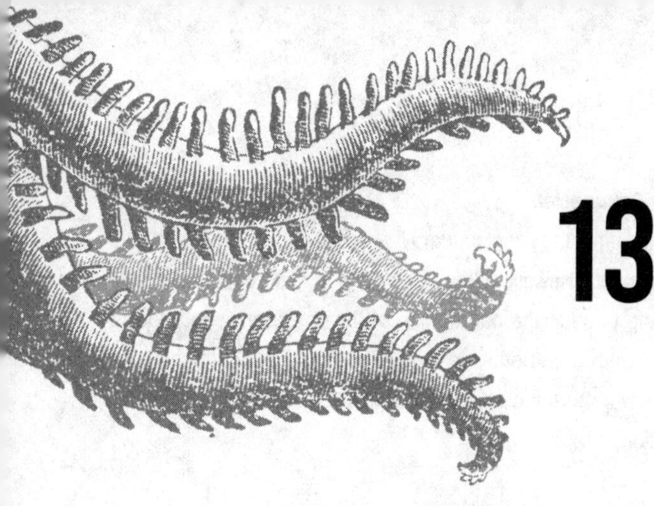

13

Passive Actions, Required Agents

Age of Expansion

The Star Eaters controlled the meridian element until the attack by Rakyir and Dossania. This marked the end of the Age of Expansion.

Age of Dissolution

The War of Dissolution began when the Rakyir Polity and the States of Dossania launched an invasion against the Star Eaters with the purpose of gaining control of the meridian element. The war quickly spiraled as other powers moved to protect their interests. It dragged until the Star Eaters had been brought to the brink of extinction, causing a state of crisis.

An urgent agreement was formed to prevent further catastrophe, resulting in the formation of the conglomerate, the first universal decision-making body. It was deemed vital to galactic interests to place the reduced Star Eater population in a regimented, protected environment, as well as to force the distribution of the meridian element into a transparent and fair arrangement.

Age of Foundation

The founding of the conglomerate marked the official end of the Age of Dissolution. However, Dissolution Era is generally accepted as extending through the devastation of the post-war period. Including the famines and other resource shortages that continued long past the war, Dissolution wiped out eighteen percent of the galactic population.

Age of Balance

The Age of Balance saw a period of smoothness and growth as the galaxy's civilizations were able to develop beyond post-war recovery. The conglomerate was proving a successful experiment in maintaining peace across all people.

Several activist movements arose during this time that argued for alteration of the Star Eaters' status, but none gained traction.

Age of Labor

Activism surrounding the Star Eaters began to gain widespread popular support, and their controlled existence began to be seen as a crime against morality. Much commentary at the time issued dire warnings that emancipation could lead to the Star Eaters' subsequent disappearance and the collapse of galactic civilization. However, they were granted full conglomerate membership near the end of the Age of Labor.

Since then, the Star Eaters have overall maintained an identical status quo, satisfied with their defined role in the conglomerate.

—"A Timeline of Dissolution," excerpted from
state-sanctioned curriculum materials issued in
the Khord Confederation and its protectorates

"This is lucky. You are lucky!" Mother Hobi railed at Ro, once his own artificial world had been extinguished and they were alone in the Orro astral pocket, centered within the walls of Ro's cell.

He'd extricated himself from You-Outside and scurried away from the bulkhead, desperate for his hive mother's comfort and advice. Diving toward her like a guiding star.

Instead, her reaction made him want to stop existing.

Stop feeling. Stop remembering. Wake from this nightmare of his own making.

He had never seen her like this. Never even heard her raise her voice.

IT'S NOT RIGHT, THAT THEY BLAME SOMEONE ELSE, Ro tried to insist again, but the words were barely a twitch.

"Do not misplace your sympathy! Chances are this worker was stealing meridian. Some have!" Mother Hobi snapped.

Like Orro wanted me to do, thought Ro.

"You are *well aware* of how simple the Star Eaters are to manipulate, or you should be. They are prone to doing anything asked by the conglomerate! Your *friend* would have been easily fooled into believing something an official request; this is a known and common problem. It's likely why the Overseers were watching her in the first place!"

Watching You-In-Front. Not Ro. Mother Hobi had assumed so from Ro's first description; Ro hadn't even considered the possibility.

WHOEVER ASKED HER SHOULD BE PUNISHED, THEN, he said. NOT THE WORKER.

"This is the reality we live in. It is the reality you refuse to live in, but you *must*!" Mother Hobi reared, her claws tearing the air. "The conglomerate has *never* played fair when it comes to meridian distribution. It's why Orro needs to make its own equality!"

By joining the corruption.

"The only thing that may save you with the Warren and the Primaries—the *only* thing—is if this *does not fall on you*. Your life, the lives of all on Orro, all could be forfeit, how can I make you see!"

Tears had begun to leak from both corners of each eye. Ro had never seen Mother Hobi cry.

She'd weathered Warren politics all her life. She was one of the most accomplished in his hive.

She was terrified for him.

Half of him wanted to rush to reassure her, apologize again, promise he was listening.

The other half wanted to demand how many moral compromises they were willing to make. How many was too many, how many to balance his life, his family's lives . . .

How many . . .

How many. He'd had the thought in Star Eater.

QUOTA, Ro whispered.

"What did you say?" demanded Mother Hobi. "Ro!"

QUOTA, Ro said. He felt as if a whole collector fleet had barreled into him. THEY KEPT SAYING 'QUOTA.' I PUT IT IN MY REPORT—

"This is not the time for your—"

IT'S A MINDSET! Ro spoke over her. QUOTA IS A MINDSET. IT'S THE MAXIMAL 'HOW MUCH' OR 'HOW MANY,' BUT ALL THE INTERROGATIVES AND DEMONSTRATIVES CONFLATE.

QUOTA IS A WHAT AND A WHY, BECAUSE WHAT AND WHY IS A 'HOW MUCH' . . .

All the gestures felt close enough to be synonymous, as if he were saying the same word over and over again.

Without context, they *were* the same word. Or near enough. This wasn't only a matter of Ro's imperfect fluency, but something deeper—some linguistic relation they hadn't yet considered—

Quota wasn't a number; *meeting quota* was an attitude. An attitude of accumulation, as *how much* also meant *what much* and *why much* and *because much*.

That tickle in his mind, during his conversation with You-Outside—he'd been so fraught, he hadn't paid attention, but it was exploding, unfolding in his mind—

THE BODY KNOWS WHEN. Ro said the words like they might shatter. WE TRANSLATE IT TO MEAN *WHEN-WHAT-TIME*. WHY DO WE TRANSLATE IT THAT WAY? WHO SAID IT MEANT *WHEN*?

Mother Hobi's face had gone slack and stricken.

HAS ANY STAR EATER EXPLAINED? Ro asked. OR DID ONE SCHOLAR TRANSLATE IT, AND EVERYONE ELSE REPEATED, EVERYONE REPEATED IT . . .

"It cannot be," Mother Hobi said. The exposed skin against her eyes and nostrils had gone nearly white.

IT MIGHT NOT BE 'WHEN,' Ro pushed, babbling now, but he couldn't stop. IT COULD BE 'HOW MUCH' OR 'WHERE,' BUT THE TIMING WORDS ARE MOST CONFLATED WITH METHOD WORDS, IT COULD BE—

Mother Hobi's mouth barely moved. "The body knows how."

THE STAR EATERS HAVE GENETIC MEMORY, Ro said.

The body knows how.

The idea that Star Eater genetic memory applied only to meridian instincts, that was just a guess, wasn't it, nobody knew for sure, it might be part of other processes, too . . .

Which meant if Ro could get one of the other Star Eaters to guide him, to jog that process like with mining—this was why relationships mattered, this was why *language* mattered, he'd had the right priorities all along! If he could use that, if he could keep building those connections, he would only need one willing instructor—

I could have young.

For Orro. For everyone.

Mother Hobi and her astral pocket blinked out.

And everything after that went so fast it blurred.

The astral orb had vanished, leaving Ro disoriented and alone. He had barely begun processing what had happened—what he might have discovered—when the field barriers on the cells buzzed and turned off. Overseers wound down the grid, ordering them out, to the ore center, all three shifts, *now now now now* . . .

Ro hustled along with the others. By the time the workers came to assemble, the conglomerate was waiting.

Ro had never heard such a thing described. Had never imagined it. The astral pockets from the orbs had expanded and overlapped, rippling out to wash over the workers and Overseers to envelop them all: a thin, nearly monochrome field showing every representative who wanted to be seen or heard. Legged beings and finned beings and amorphous beings, in textiles or exoskeletons or illusion clouds, some with gravity collars or containment fields or symbiotes. A shimmering liquid person, a crawling swarm, several that seemed to be something in between. For one representative, an enormous compound eye was all that shone from their part of the astral field.

Ro couldn't have said how he knew, so unfamiliar were so many of the species, but every translucent ghost frowned angry and unfriendly upon them.

The Overseers corralled the last of the workers inside—all three shifts together, crowded up against one side of the ore center in an uneasy, tentacled mass. One Overseer dragged in You-In-Front, its coils constricting against her membranes and cilia. She twitched within its confines, largely unhurt but pulsing with a frantic fear. Its metallic swaddle had knotted her within a serpentine stranglehold until she was barely able to move.

Ro had a sudden visceral image of why the Overseers had been designed as they had.

He tried to shut out where the rest of the automata clanked and swam among the grid behind the workers, a continuous menace.

A fleeting moment of gratitude struck, that Ro had relayed his revelation to Orro already. If this was about to collapse on him, if the conglomerate was here to render judgment—at least Orro knew what he'd discovered. And another part of him howled in absurd impatience, because his crimes that had felt so dire mere moments ago paled in importance next to the idea of *Star Eater young*, and he needed to research and see—

Then Mother Hobi stepped forward, a small, furred glow in the eerie translucence of the merged astral field.

"We have discovered your secret," she said.

She was speaking Hark, one of the most common trade

languages in the galaxy. That must be why her words seemed to spit through her teeth.

"You have been lying to us for age upon age," Mother Hobi snarled. "Orro has informed our brethren of the other domains. The conglomerate calls upon you to answer for your duplicity!"

She wasn't looking at Ro. It belatedly occurred to him that a much larger, more obvious question was not whether he himself could produce a budded Star Eater or two.

It was why none of the others had.

No. Oh, no.

"Why have you purposely withheld your next generation?" Mother Hobi demanded. Her voice reverberated through the collective astral field they shared, across the ore center and the crowd and its vigilant Overseers. "This is a conspiracy to destroy us. You would murder countless worlds for your revenge!"

Not a move from the Star Eaters, not a word. Not a twitch.

"Overseer, force one to answer!" The order boomed from the enormous blunt face of an atmospheric whale, one who must speak for one of the gas giants.

The Overseer holding You-In-Front lashed farther around her body and squeezed. She beat out a gasp of pain, the ends of her appendages jerking in tics.

STOP IT! STOP! Ro cried, but nobody was looking at him.

"These connivers would not have allowed such a process to be lost," boomed the whale. "They must be preserving and recollecting it in secret. They guard its power and wait out our demise!"

The Star Eaters' own lack of concern reinforced such

an accusation, Ro realized with a sinking anguish. They would have known the correct meaning all along . . . if they had lost the vital knowledge, either to confusion or time, they would have been desperate to regain it.

Indifference only fit if it was a deliberate ploy.

UNTRUE, UNTRUE, You-In-Front pleaded, muffled to weak twitches in the Overseer's fisted embrace. I DON'T KNOW WHAT YOU SPEAK OF!

"You can have young!" Mother Hobi's claws whipped to point at her in clear indictment. "We have checked the historical translation. You can. You refuse!"

OUR BODIES KNOW WHEN! You-In-Front's words had lost intelligibility around the edges. THE BODY KNOWS WHEN, WE CANNOT—I DON'T KNOW—

"The insult!" shrieked Mother Hobi. "You mock us in plain sight. You know *how*, you just said it yourself!"

DON'T KNOW, WE DON'T! You-In-Front wailed out. The Overseer's coils slid over each other, twisting tighter. THE BODIES KNOW WHEN, WHAT TIME. THE CHOOSING, IT CANNOT BE DONE BY US. YOU SAY THIS WHY!

Her sentences were garbling, but oddly, like she kept accidentally saying the ending before the beginning. Ro had done that before when he talked too fast or unfocused in Red Top or Lower Senti—they swapped their word order opposite from Ponto or Star Eater, verb first, everything else at the end, and it didn't matter because they were going to kill his friend and Ro was going to have to watch and *why was he noticing*—

KNOW NOTHING. KNOW NOTHING, You-In-Front shuddered, over and over, making an extra flattened gesture with some of her ends.

Not a native Star Eater motion. A loanword, no, a borrowed affectation—Ro hated himself for the way the trivia came to mind, but at the same time, something about this felt important, something . . . Even though nothing had ever been less important in his life . . . The gesture was from an oral culture, wasn't it, one with several bipedal species, but which? Like the Ponto rolled claws or the Nahonic clasped hands, it held a meaning of submissive pleading or prayer—

In Lower Senti.

You-In-Front's word order. Her slang.

If the Star Eaters knew the right translation, their indifference had no explanation but pretense—unless—*unless*—

WAIT. STOP! Ro cried.

He hurled himself into the center of the assembly, swinging himself around by his bracers to skid directly between You-In-Front and Mother Hobi. The attention of an angry conglomerate creaked over onto him like a teetering rockfall. Mother Hobi gazed at him in horror, but she couldn't say anything, couldn't stop him.

THIS ONE IS TELLING THE TRUTH! Ro shouted. SHE DOESN'T KNOW, SHE REALLY DOESN'T, SHE'S A JUMPER!

The crowd went silent as an empty world.

They wouldn't all use the same word for it. But they would know.

They would know.

Ro searched among the representatives' avatars, the bulbous faces and compound eyes and fins and swarms and wings, to find a fragile, pale bipedal and spindle frame five times the height of a Ponto, in the flowing clothed fashions of Lower Senti.

I'M RIGHT, AREN'T I? Ro's motions were cracked and brittle. YOU CAN JUMP TOO. YOU CAN JUMP TOO . . .

The rapid drift. The muddy morphosyntax. The broken collocations, the adpositions, the loanwords and calques and borrowed slang, and everyone so nervous of being targeted yet never wanting to leave . . .

The confusion periods. The jumbled deixis. The loss of discourse markers, so difficult for second language speakers, and the question words, the question words, so blurred into each other that nobody could possibly discern them . . . unless everyone was pretending to.

The thinness of opinion, of culture, as every Star Eater always said . . . what *everybody else expected* a Star Eater to say . . .

Ro spun in space, no way up. His wheeling senses sought out the other Star Eaters—the Star Eaters who weren't Star Eaters at all.

ALL OF YOU. IT'S ALL OF YOU . . .

"*Stop!*" Mother Hobi flung a claw at Ro, and it took him a moment to register she had reverted to Ponto by accident, so great her agitation. "This creature has a sickness; detain her. She lies!"

The type of lie she accused him of was the worst of them all. *A targeted, devious lie. One meant to distort what is felt or real.*

Ro's hearts broke.

Both of the hearts he no longer had, the hearts he'd given up, all to know a people who no longer existed.

The Overseers' heads swiveled toward him but didn't grasp the command. Mother Hobi hadn't caught on yet that it didn't matter what Orro secrets he spilled, because nothing was secret, nothing was hidden, nothing was real.

WE'RE ALL FROM OTHER WORLDS, AREN'T WE. Ro flung it forth before another order could be given, before any automaton could pounce. His words tripped over each other, a jerking thrash against the tableau. THE MORPHOSYNTAX, LOOK AT THE MORPHOSYNTAX . . . THE LOST INFLECTIONS, THE DISCOURSE MARKERS, NONE OF US ARE NATIVE SPEAKERS, TELL ME I'M WRONG, TELL ME I'M WRONG . . .

Everything in Ro was dissolving apart, liquifying and shriveling to nothing.

The Star Eater population had been so small. How many times had each of their minds been overwritten, then overwritten again, by a spy for another people? So many times, so many eras, each parroting a culture none of them understood. Imitating their own invented expectations, until it all flattened to a single note.

Did any of the conglomerate know? Or did they tell themselves, like Orro, that they stole only a life or three per generation?

In the absence of more orders, the Overseer's grip on You-In-Front had loosened, and her frills opened like petals, a stunned realization of tragedy.

IS IT TRUE? she whispered.

YOU'RE FROM LOWER SENTI, AREN'T YOU? Ro had to push himself to say the next part, so embedded was the need for secrecy, but he was right, he was right and everything else was wrong. I'M PONTO. FROM ORRO.

The stillness was like the breath before an earthquake.

Then You-Behind moved, from the redward side of Ro. KHORD, she said, the motion nearly imperceptible. THE KHORD CONFEDERATION.

Of course.

SO WAS THIS BODY, BEFORE ME, Ro guessed. Another Linguist, one Ro had unintentionally echoed. YOU BOTH JUMPED.

You-Behind gave the barest motion of assent. Ro had replaced the only being here who knew her true person.

How many of them had sailed in on the confused minds of other spies? None had been jumping in over Star Eaters, only pasting one spy over another—

VALLAMUNG, spoke up another worker then. I'M FROM VALLAMUNG.

FAR NARANYU, said another. WE WERE SUPPOSED TO BE THE ONLY ONES . . .

Two more gestured from the back—THE ALLIANCE SYSTEM.

Then more and more and more, speaking over each other, drawing strength from the crowd, domains Ro had heard of and ones he hadn't.

Some of the conglomerate representatives had begun to react, its oral majority rising in shouts. Denial and rejection and commands to the Overseers in too many tongues, jumbled and contradictory.

IS ANYONE? You-In-Front asked, and others took up the call, even those who hadn't volunteered other origins.

ANYONE?

ANYONE?

ANYONE?

Ro joined in. ANYONE? IS ANYONE STILL A STAR EATER?

A gestural language never had to compete with sound. The workers' chorus of movement fell in sync, the same desperate question.

The protests from the conglomerate aborted and died.

Every mining ship would undergo some sort of census, every mind catalogued, but Ro knew what it would show.

WE KILLED THEM, he said into the quiet. WE KILLED THEM ALL.

Fewer than three lives in a generation, they'd told themselves at the Warren. Worth the sacrifice. To understand, and learn, and help their people.

Collectively, a genocide.

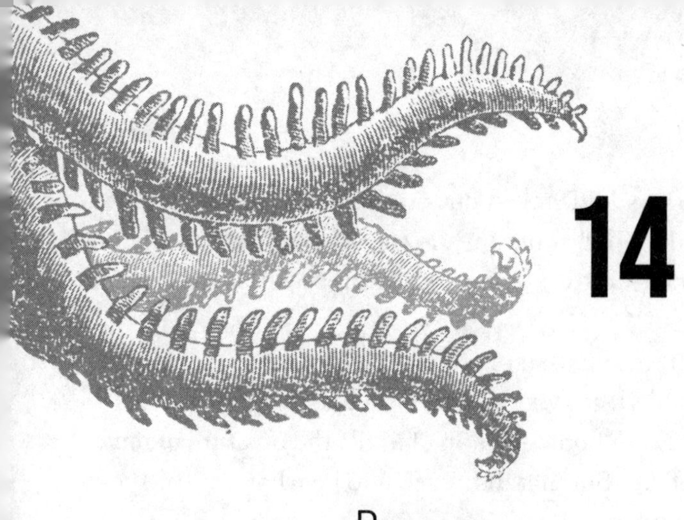

14

Reverse, Repair, Redeem—

Why does ANYONE get tizzed over Star Eater 'rights'? They haven't stood up for themselves once since they lost at Dissolution! THEY DON'T FOOKIN CARE. It was all these smash-hearted overcompensating fixers who wanted to do anything in the first place, stirring your drama pots and insisting they get their precious freedom. Well you got your way centuries ago and guess what, they didn't give a flip. And now you want us to protest about conditions or reparations or whatevers, but you can't even get the space squids themselves to be mad about it? Lemme lay it on you: THEY LIKED BEING SLAVES.

—Paw de Holmsheed, Accordance Age
political commentator, unaffiliated

I MISS FORESTS, murmured You-In-Front. AT HOME THE TREES GREW TALLER THAN ANY SKY TOWER. YOU COULD LIE AND GAZE UP AND NEVER SEE WHERE THEY ENDED.

She and Ro drifted together in one of the sections

the workers had staked out on the now-docked collector, where they had waited while the scholars and mediators descended and the conglomerate representatives wailed denial.

IT SOUNDS BEAUTIFUL, Ro said. PEACEFUL.

DO YOU THINK WE CAN EVER GO BACK?

Star Eater bodies couldn't handle the pressure of much atmosphere. But that didn't seem to be what You-In-Front was asking.

MAYBE, Ro said. He didn't know what had happened to his own body. IF ALL THE LINGUISTS FROM ALL THE GOVERNMENTS KEEP POOLING THEIR KNOWLEDGE . . . THERE MIGHT BE SOME WAY TO JUMP BACK.

That wasn't the real question, either.

THEY'RE NOT STILL INSIDE US, ARE THEY? You-In-Front said. IF WE COULD . . .

Ro wanted to believe there was a chance. He'd extinguish his own consciousness in a heartbeat if it meant giving this body back to the one it belonged to. But the scholars had already dismissed that possibility.

None of them could go back. Not in the way they needed.

I HEARD THEY FIGURED OUT IT'S ONLY THE STAR EATER NEUROLOGY THAT MADE IT POSSIBLE, You-In-Front said. WE MIGHT BE . . . THIS WAY TILL THE END. FOR A LONG TIME.

The Star Eater lifetime. Centuries or even millennia, when not overwritten by another mind.

Centuries in a stolen body, everything scraped from it save form and shell.

The Warren had always claimed the linguistic jumps were a sacred skill of the Ponto empathic sense. Ro wondered if they'd believed it. In hindsight, that Star Eater mental ability to slide into the meridian dimension seemed an obvious candidate for explaining how it worked.

But few people had known of the jumps at all, and enough had simply accepted.

Had other governments stolen the skill from Orro, or Orro from them? History that far back blended to mist, and today's politicians were spinning into blame and truth-washing as they pointed responsibility off themselves. It might never be known which domains had independently developed the ability, versus who had gained it through espionage. Clearly none of those who used it had any qualms with spying.

IF HAVING OFFSPRING WAS GENETIC MEMORY, AND NONE OF US HAVE IT . . . You-In-Front said.

I KNOW, Ro answered.

No one could manufacture knowledge that was simply gone.

With the process of their reproduction a lost genetic memory, the would-be Star Eaters had no way to guide each other to its mechanisms. The species would die in body as well as mind.

Much of civilization would follow.

THERE'S STILL TIME, Ro said.

NOT FOR THEM.

They were quiet for a moment.

WE ENDED THEIR PEOPLE, You-In-Front said. WE WIPED THEM OUT.

WORSE. Ro's body tried to curve toward a protective claw-curl, a mimicry of when he was Ponto. WE OVERWROTE THEM. EVERYTHING THEY ARE. EVERYTHING WE KNOW OF THEIR CULTURE . . .

A shallow construct, mashed together from strangers' assumptions.

He'd only wanted to understand them. How many Linguists had told themselves that lie? *A lie enough repeated until it becomes true.*

How many had convinced themselves that stealing a culture, a language, a mind, was warranted by the noble yearning of scholarly study? How many had eagerly participated in that erasing, with only the seemingly minor act of inserting themselves? Others had reached for justifications that they were saving civilization, saving their worlds . . .

So many lies.

The entire Star Eater culture had been turned lie. One the Ponto language didn't have a word big enough for.

WHAT WILL WE DO? You-In-Front asked. Pleading. WHAT WILL WE DO NOW?

Continue mining was the obvious answer. If they left, people would die. Worlds would die.

Ro wasn't sure that meant they should stay.

Would the conglomerate let them do otherwise? So many ages of the Star Eaters staying and working and doing everything the conglomerate governments asked, because every single one was an agent of those governments . . . The galaxy had never truly had to wrestle with giving freedom to workers whose motives might stray from its own.

Maybe Ro and the others would begin choosing differently from each other, now that they weren't imitating ghosts. Maybe the meridian element would be taken over by the government who'd had the most spies.

Maybe there'd be another war.

Ro couldn't stir himself to much emotion for that, not when the worst had already happened.

WHAT'S YOUR NAME? You-In-Front asked.

She marked the interrogative with an awkward overclarity, something most of them had started doing without discussion. Ro responded with the oralization phonetics that had been constructed in Star Eater, spelling out an alveolar approximant followed by a close-mid back rounded vowel with sliding tone. Not everyone would know the oralization alphabet, with its hundreds of signs approximating the sounds of every species, far beyond standard Ponto transliterations. But a fellow Linguist would know it.

All the Star Eaters were fellow Linguists. Ro had been among his own this whole time.

WELL MET, RO. MY NAME IS JƏƱ'HANN. As was common in Lower Senti, You-In-Front hooked a gender marker to the end of the name.

YOU'RE MALE? Ro said.

I DON'T KNOW WHAT WE ARE ANYMORE, Jəʊ'hann said.

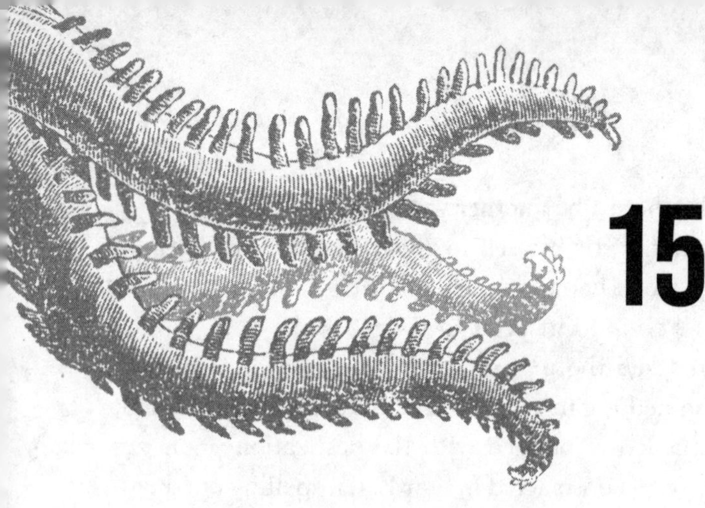

15

Causative Case, Involitive Grief, Plural Guilt

We gouged our civilization from the bodies of others while pretending to decency. Yet we gasp in surprise when we receive so flawlessly what we have earned.

—the poet Rugauk, post-revelations

I'm just gonna come out and say it, this is hornslag. Not one of us regular folk did anything. It was government secrets a hundred layers above and ancestors a hundred eras behind, and now we get to drink their poison while the ministers and kings ride the last of the meridian somewhere safe.

—anonymous commenter, post-revelations

I'm not crying for us. I'm crying for the Star Eaters. I'm crying because we never even knew their name.

—celebrity activator Pi Pi Půreidz, post-revelations

Ro left.

Nearly half the Star Eaters left—the Star Eaters who weren't Star Eaters at all. Some sought closeness with their original homeworlds. Others refused to say where they were going. Ro worried that some might seek a premature end, a cessation of the guilt and devastated purpose. He would likely never know.

Bearing what their people had done, what *they* had done . . . bearing it every day, in a stolen body that would last for an eternity of lifespans . . .

The heaviness deserved to crush them.

In the wake of the departing miners, the conglomerate was left squabbling, metaphorically scratching out each others' entrails. Word had leaked to the public and across the other mining ships too fast to forcibly keep the workers in service, had any governments been malicious enough to intend such or cooperative enough with each other to plan it. Ro decided to depart before they could.

The revelations rippled out through a horrified galaxy, one now facing accelerated disaster. While their representatives melted down or pushed petty blame, the public exploded with the sorts of opinions civilized people can have when they see the end of that civilization bearing down but have not yet lived it.

Ro got messages from a dozen in his hive, including his litter-sisters and Lalo. All had doubtless been sent his way by Mother Hobi. They lavished him with emotion and begged him to stay with the mining ships. Pleading that Orro would be among the first to die without the meridian element.

They were likely correct.

Orro would have to find a place to become refugees. Somewhere with more self-sufficiency, when such places would be packed to engorgement and far too many others would be asking.

Seven million Orro refugees.

Ro couldn't fix it. He couldn't fix it by staying. Nobody could fix it.

Philosophers across the galaxy might argue paths toward their collective moral redemption, or technologists theorize undiscovered ways to evade the coming consequences. But sometimes history broke things enough that the living couldn't fix them.

Ro understood that now.

He turned away from the messages and left.

Jəʊ'hann came with him, as did a handful of the others, none of whom Ro had known on his collector. You-Outside had professed a desire to go home, though Ro didn't know if she could—her true homeworld was an aquatic one. As for You-Behind, Ro hadn't seen her since that explosive gathering with the conglomerate. He hoped she was all right, wherever she was. Khord was not known for its gentleness—requiring its spies to experiment on themselves was unlikely to have been its worst command.

More drifting threads he would never find answers to.

Ro's own plans had the sketchiness of shadows. They amounted to one faint, desperate hope: *Reconstruct the Star Eaters.*

Their language, their culture, their identity. THEY DESERVE TO BE REMEMBERED AS THEY TRULY WERE, he insisted, over and over. WHATEVER AMENDS WE CAN MAKE, WE MUST.

The selfish, unspoken reason was that Ro needed this. Bad enough to live in a body he'd abducted . . . He needed some way to at least attempt its truth.

WHERE DO WE START? Jəʊ'hann asked. Ro still had trouble not thinking of him as You-In-Front. Jəʊ'hann had started wearing colorful textile scarves reminiscent of Lower Senti fashion, which looked odd and made his words harder to understand, but nobody commented. Some of the others were doing similar: body painting for the spy from New Gekku, or linked and knotted jewelry for the one from the Schuya Republic, which made a rhythmic music when they spoke.

RECORDS, Ro said. WE FIND ALL THE RECORDS WE CAN. AND WHEN THEY SPEAK, WE LISTEN.

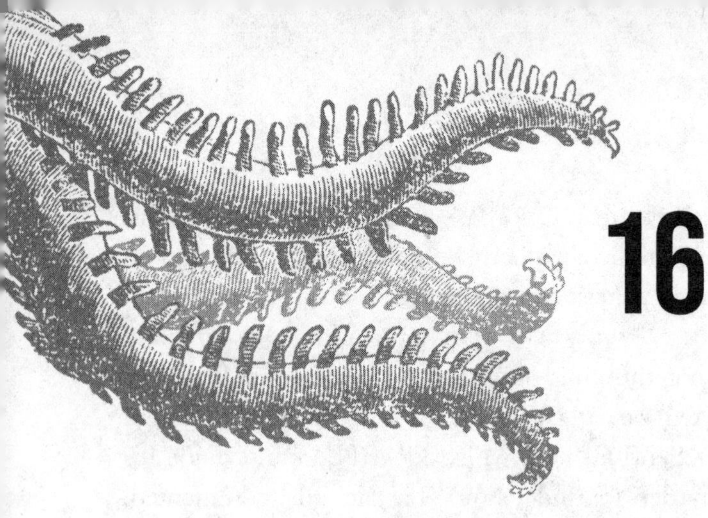

16

Epilogue: The Stories We Tell. The Stories We Steal.

As on the first four markings of this anniversary, on this fifth one I will attempt to release our findings, though once again I warn of their sparsity. As before, we have made every attempt to insert neither lens nor bias while simultaneously building enough context for the non-scholar to come away without erroneous conclusions. We've surely failed. As yet, however, this remains the most consistent and primary-sourced compendium of research into the historical truth of those we called the Star Eaters, and we encourage others to build upon this work. Or simply to read it, and remember them.

—"On Those We Called the Star Eaters,"
Sequence 5. Ro et al.

WE'RE NEVER GOING TO MANAGE IT, ARE WE, Jəʊ'hann said. WE'LL NEVER FIND WHO THEY REALLY WERE.

Ro didn't want to answer.

They drifted in an orbital research station that had

been backed by activists, ones who spent most of their time quarreling loudly on the nexus about how much blame for the Star Eaters' extinction ought to be borne by ordinary citizens. The group largely used their involvement with Ro's project to win arguments and otherwise left them alone. Ro and the others did their work in a capsule anchored to a young, uninhabited rock within a sparse nebula that met the Star Eaters' basic needs, and nobody bothered them—but nor was their work at the forefront of a desperate galaxy's priorities.

As the conglomerate sniped at each other and tilted on its stilts, the raw resource shortage had already begun creeping in on the farthest reaches of the meridian paths. Seventeen austerity measures had gone into effect from different governments. Ro was conscious that their research station might someday go dark too, as reserves bled toward maintaining survival.

Eventually, they might be forced out into the nebula to live as the Star Eater ancients had.

Only five of their original group remained. Some of the departed had returned to the mining ships, driven by guilt or an ache for the numb and familiar. Others, failing to find what they craved with Ro and his people, had left to seek it elsewhere.

Ro would have too if he'd known anywhere else.

Still others had wondered if what their group sought didn't risk replacing one damage with another. *Do we have the right?* they'd asked, and Ro had no answer. Any action risked further injury, and so did taking no action at all.

Ro chose faith where he could find meaning, and lived

every day with the awareness that he didn't know what was right.

The little they'd found might be too scant for impact anyway. Like dust on a breeze.

THERE'S NOT ENOUGH LEFT, Jəʊ'hann continued, in weary resignation. He stretched, arching, into a cloud of celeon sensory gas. Ro had been encouraging the others to explore—sense experiences and stimulations that might re-find what the Star Eaters had enjoyed before their long stretch of oppression.

The group had attempted to pinpoint when the grasping replacements by other civilizations had begun. It had been long before the Star Eaters were freed, as even then, having spies in their midst would have allowed for the corrupt reappropriation of meridian. By the time the rest of the galaxy deigned to wonder about their miners as sentient beings again, the reality of who they were had been eclipsed.

Fading into a forgotten history.

NO, Ro said reluctantly. THERE'S NOT ENOUGH LEFT.

ONLY SCRATCHES ON THE PAINT OF THE PAST, Jəʊ'hann said. SHADOWS AND ECHOES, ONCE WE RUBBED THEM ALL AWAY.

Jəʊ'hann had been experimenting with poetry in the Star Eater language. Some of it would have made Ro cry, if he still had tears.

Ro left the edge of one appendage listening to the vibrations of database upon database and scooted closer to Jəʊ'hann, his membranes opening to the soothing caress of the celeon. They drifted close to each other, almost touching.

Ponto and Lower Senti were both tactile cultures. All experiments in intertwining as Star Eaters had ended in gooey discomfort and stinging irritation, even through protective sleeves.

Ro missed touching people. They both did.

THERE MUST HAVE BEEN A FEW REAL ONES LEFT AT THE TIME THEIR RIGHTS WERE RETURNED, Ro said. A FEW WERE BORN AFTER THEN. ASSUMING ONLY THE REAL STAR EATERS COULD REPRODUCE . . .

DO YOU THINK THEY KNEW WHAT WAS HAPPENING? Jəʊ'hann asked. EVERYONE AROUND THEM DEVELOPING NEUROSES AND AMNESIA, MIND AFTER MIND, AND NO ONE WOULD LISTEN . . . A DEMENTIA OF OPPRESSION. A GRADUAL DROWNING OF THE SELF AND SOUL THAT WOULD SOMEDAY TAKE THEM ALL.

IT DID TAKE THEM ALL, Ro said. *We took them all.*

Something tickled the preoccupied ends of his cilia, the ones that were still reading.

MAYBE THEY DID KNOW, he said.

Jəʊ'hann contracted in surprise, his scarves and sleeves drifting behind the motion. WHAT? WHAT DID YOU FIND?

THESE POPULATION RECORDS. Ro read back, then forward, then back again, reiterating the calculation request. IT'S NOT . . . IT'S NOT CLEAR, BUT SOME MIGHT BE MISSING?

SOME WHAT? SOME WHO?

Ro's momentary hope ebbed back down. THE RECORDS ARE FRAGMENTARY. PROBABLY JUST LOST.

BUT SOME MIGHT HAVE RUN?

Or it might be Ro's wishful thinking. Like so many other times.

A TALE OF DARING ESCAPE, Jəʊ'hann murmured. One of

his scarves brushed Ro's cilia, a gentle tease. DAGGERS ON ALL SIDES, AS EVERY MIND AROUND THEM GOES DEAD AND STRANGE. THEY TAKE THEIR CHILDREN AND DISAPPEAR INTO THE BLACK FROM WHICH THEY CAME. THEY KNOW THE VASTNESS OF THE UNIVERSE—NO ONE CAN SEARCH THAT MUCH EMPTY SPACE. THEY CAN STAY LOST, AS LONG AS THEY CHOOSE NEVER TO SPEAK.

A tantalizing story.

A tantalizing fiction, that some Star Eaters might have fled into the vacuum, restarting a parallel civilization to thrive in undiscovered nebulae. Jəʊ'hann was right—if they went silent and never made contact, they would never be found.

If they had done such a thing, they would have known they were condemning the rest of the galaxy. He wouldn't blame them if they'd thought it justice.

They could have been deliberate about hiding from the interlopers how to have young. Perhaps they figured they owed nothing. Least of all their children.

The rest of the galaxy could figure itself out.

The rest of the galaxy wasn't going to. Scholars' estimates of the coming first wave of casualties started in the billions.

The story Jəʊ'hann had spun was one Ro yearned to find possible. But it wasn't any more true than any other story they'd engraved over the Star Eaters, tales that only had one thing in common . . . that their storytellers wanted to believe them.

IT WILL NEVER BE ENOUGH, WILL IT? Jəʊ'hann asked, leaning in with a closeness that let Ro feel his warm disturbance on the swirling celeon. WHAT IS OUR HOPE? EVEN IF

WE FOUND FRAGMENTS OF THEIR INNERMOST WORLDS, WE WILL ONLY BE DOING MORE OF THE SAME . . . PLACING OURSELVES INSIDE THEIR MOUTHS AND PRETENDING TO TRUTH.

Ro could remember a time when he hadn't understood: That was what it meant, to study another people.

That was always what it meant.

What *did* they hope for? When there was no fixing, no solving? When the crisis swallowing their universe and the tragedy they were complicit in were both impossible in their enormity?

No answer would be adequate. What could anyone hope for?

A SMALLER LIE, Ro said. THAT'S WHAT WE HAVE. A SMALLER LIE.

ACKNOWLEDGMENTS

My warmest thanks to the incredible team who helped me bring this book to life. My agent, Russ Galen, ensured the space was created for me to write it in the first place, which was less than straightforward during a difficult time in my career. I then brought this idea to my editor at Tor, Oliver Dougherty, because I knew they would be the ideal match for it—and their overwhelming support became a greenhouse for the themes I wanted to explore. Additional thanks, and some apologies, are due to my film agent, Angela Cheng Caplan, who as of this writing has already requested a copy of what I'm sure is the most unfilmable book I've ever written (sorry!!).

The professionals who worked with me through Tor on this book's design and production have also been unparalleled. I was blown away by my cover artist, Pablo Delcan, and am thrilled with the finished piece completed by jacket designer Shreya Gupta. The interior design of this book has offered more complication than average, and interior designer Heather Saunders has gone above and beyond with attentiveness and detail.

My copyeditor Bailey Harrington deserves particular mention for such shining thoroughness and discussion, whether on science or linguistics or my knotted-up world-building. Working with Bailey and with production editor Dakota Griffin has truly been a joy. More gratitude as well goes to my managing editor Lauren Hougen, production manager Jim Kapp, editorial intern J Tronsky, proofreader Norma Hoffman, and cold reader Sam Dauer, who complete this book's editorial powerhouse.

It's also my honor to continue with the marketing and publicity team that has so enthusiastically boosted prior books for me at Tor, including lead marketer Isa Caban, lead publicist Giselle Gonzalez, and social media manager Sam Friedlander. Here's to many more!

Outside of Tor, I am eternally grateful to my sister and to Ellison Hyde, who both blew past any reasonable generosity with their time and feedback. This book had such tight complexities that I sometimes despaired I could ever make its many fragile gears fit. May every writer have a support system like them to help see the sweat and tears through.

My writing communities—with far too many lovely people to list—were also indispensable, with their willingness to hop in on brainstorming threads or language questions or to give me an opinion on tentacle design. I have been additionally humbled by the wider community of readers and the amount of early support this book has received, from excited shout-outs online to my early-bird blurbists—it has been quite meaningful, and thank you for making the journey surprising and extraordinary.

My other friends, family, and communities are more than a person could ever reasonably hope for, both in writing and in life. I am profoundly lucky to have all of you.

Finally, in the wider world, I would be remiss if I did not give a call out to Ed Yong's science nonfiction book *An Immense World*, as the unimagined and bizarre truths of our own planet served as such fertile inspiration for my alien sensory details. I would further like to highlight the countless teachers, professors, lecturers, authors, translators, podcasters, and friends who have fed my layman's keenness for linguistics and language over the years, including the numerous patient and welcoming instructors of Spanish, Chinese, Japanese, Italian, Latin, and ASL who have expanded my multilingual world here on Earth. Most of all, to the activists and thinkers among that group who have driven a reckoning with how the joy of science and learning can and should be irrevocably tangled with questions of respect and humanity—to the preservers and protectors of language, of culture, and most importantly of people—thank you. I am deeply grateful for that work, as a multicultural person, as a scholar, and as a human being in the world.

ABOUT THE AUTHOR

Chris Massa, Chris Massa Photography

S. L. Huang is a Hollywood stunt performer, firearms expert, and Hugo Award winner who has been a finalist for the Nebula, Locus, and BSFA Awards as well as the ALA Carnegie Medal. Huang has a math degree from MIT and credits in productions like *Battlestar Galactica* and *Top Shot.* The author of *The Water Outlaws*, *Burning Roses*, and the Cas Russell novels, Huang's short fiction has also appeared in *Analog Science Fiction & Fact*, *The Magazine of Fantasy & Science Fiction*, *Strange Horizons*, *Nature*, *Reactor*, and more, including numerous best-of anthologies.